PRAISE

"Sarah Day's debut novella captivates from the very first page; like all the best monster stories, *Greyhowler* also explores the monsters inside of us."
– Tim Pratt, author of *Prison of Sleep*

GREYHOWLER

This book is published by Underland Press, which is part of Firebird Creative, LLC (Clackamas, OR).

Let those among you who the gods' gifts elevate reach back and lift all folk beside them in turn . . .

Edited by Mark Teppo
Book Design and Layout by Firebird Creative

Underland Press
www.underlandpress.com

GREYHOWLER

SARAH DAY

Underland Press

For Bradburn

If this isn't nice, I don't know what is.

Rhia walked the prairie road for twenty-five days before she got to Cerretour. She spent the first four days in the company of strangers; wagons and riders and pedestrians spooling in and out of Tellemont, the dust and bustle of a major highway. Everyone was in motion, everyone carrying something: luggage or cargo or passengers or, in Rhia's case, a single sealed letter tucked into a hidden pocket in her pack. She slept along the roadside and lit her tiny fire within shouting distance of other tiny fires.

On the fifth day, she crossed an arched stone bridge over the river and the travelers around her dwindled.

On the eighth day, she might have seen one person, a dot scraped up over the horizon far ahead, visible for less than an hour, then gone.

On the ninth day, the paving ran out. From there on, her only company was the occasional flock of ground-nesting birds she startled off the prairie floor and into the roofless sky.

Meek spring seared away into summer. Her black jacket came off and went into her pack, meticulously rolled to keep it from dust. Sweat evaporated. Her pack straps creaked with salt. Her woven sun hat desiccated, releasing a wisp of sweetgrass scent. During the day, everything was dun-colored: the road, the wildlife, the smear of dust limning the horizon, the grass, her bare shoulders as they bronzed in the sun. She stopped lighting fires at night, ate cold meals, and read a book in the wobbling globe of light cast by her small tin lantern. Later, in the full dark, she was kept awake by the sounds of small animals, each movement amplified by the drying grass. When she slept, she dreamed of wildfires.

Every morning, she woke to a fingernail-scrape of apricot across the eastern horizon, picked up her pack, walked until dark, read or watched the blurring smear of stars until she fell asleep, and did it again.

Whenever a sputter of creek burped out of the hard ground, she topped off her waterskins and splashed her face. Water flickered tantalizingly at the periphery of her awareness, hidden deep in the earth below the prairie, too far and sparse for even someone with Rhia's degree of Talent to sense clearly. She could only feel the presence of water within about a quarter-mile, and the prairie was wide and dry.

She had never gone this deep inland before. Most of her deliveries took her along the main roads, or to the shipping ports that studded the coast. The delivery itself was unusual—one letter, instead of a parcel or sheaf of papers or cart of goods. The outside was sealed with a thick wax stamp and a purple ribbon banded lengthwise in silver and gold. Despite being many years outside the Temple gates, her mind still recognized that color combination as *Temple colors* . . . but the Temple rarely sent their messages by Courier. Silver and gold were also rich-people colors.

It was probably a coincidence.

She didn't know what the letter contained, but she never knew what was in the packages she carried, and after four years as a Courier, she had (mostly) trained herself out of curiosity. Confidentiality was part of what you paid for when you contracted the Three Kingdoms Courier Service to take possession of an item for you and deliver it downtown or to another province or into another kingdom or across the continent.

Occasionally it was a dangerous job, but mostly it was a boring one. Lots of walking, long hours, and little company, which she preferred. Rhia was good at her job because it gave her what she wanted—solitude, mobility, self-direction, a perpetual reason to leave. It was comforting to know there was a departure at the end of every destination, curled inside it like a shoot resting inside a seed.

On the evening of the twenty-sixth day, a scruff of darker brown broke the tawny dust on the horizon. It grew as she approached: a cluster of shabby wooden buildings, and beyond, a sweeping curve of knobby trees that suggested a waterway.

Maps of this part of the country were light on detail, but even so, she knelt in the middle of the road to spread hers out and make sure she'd read it right. A Courier didn't earn her rank by having a poor sense of direction, and it's not like there were any other nearby settlements she could be mistaking for this place . . . *But it's barely a skin tag, surely it can't be—*

Cerretour, the map insisted, and capped the word with a symbol that meant *village* or *small town*.

Rhia looked up from the map, squinting down the road. There weren't more than a couple dozen buildings, along with a few big barns and outbuildings that were probably jointly owned and used by the whole community. On one side of the settlement, crop fields were laid out in a neat grid. Beans, probably, or turnips, this time of year. On the other side, a single building, dark and square, sat alone out in the middle of the prairie. Rhia couldn't imagine what that was for.

Who would pay a Courier's rates for a delivery to this little two-horse town?

Everything was getting that honey-soaked tint that came right before sunset. The grassland around the settlement glinted. Windowpanes flared. A warm breeze lifted off the prairie floor, carrying a voice from the village—far away, too indistinct to really hear, a long sliding vowel. The tail end of a name, perhaps.

Someone's down there, at any rate. Rhia began to walk.

As she walked, a dot detached itself from the dark square building out on the prairie, and started down a connecting path toward the town. It grew into a recognizably human shape—a woman about Rhia's age, with crown of light brown hair pinned up around her head, dressed in a sweeping, wide-sleeved robe.

She saw Rhia coming and waited for her where the path and the road met.

"You're new," she said. Her voice was as soft and light as birds lifting off the prairie floor.

After weeks on the road with only the bugs, jackrabbits, and her thoughts for company, Rhia drank in the sight of another human being like water.

"Yes, hi—I'm a Courier. I have a delivery—" Rhia gestured at her uniform by way of explanation, and realized belatedly that a sleeveless white shirt and black trousers weren't much of a uniform. "I have my identification in my pack. I have a delivery for the mayor."

"The headman," the woman corrected. "Cerretour is too small for a mayor."

Of course it is. "In that case, I have a delivery for the headman."

"You're not coming from the Citadel, I take it? The High Priest didn't send you?"

"I came from Tellemont." The Citadel was two provinces away. Leagues from here. "Why?"

"*Tellemont*? That's weeks away." The woman took a fresh look at Rhia—the sweatstains, the tousled hair, the road dust on her boots. "You came all this way on foot?"

"I could have come with a wagon train, but none were scheduled and I didn't want to wait. The Hall wouldn't authorize a horse. Water's too unpredictable on the prairie."

The woman's mouth crooked into an expression that was half smile, half wince. "Tell me about it."

Faced up with Rhia, the woman was a couple inches shorter, slender, with a snub nose and the deep tan and freckles of someone who worked outdoors. Sharp blue eyes, a strong mouth. The robe was fine white linen. An appliquéd band of gold, russet, teal, and blue chased itself around the collar, cuffs, and hem.

"You're a Priest," Rhia said.

"Nearly. I'm on my roving."

In rural parts of the country, acolytes on track to becoming full Priests sometimes took a year away from their home Temple to travel, ministering in smaller towns and villages that didn't have Temples of their own.

Rhia hadn't done such a journey herself. In her experience, not many acolytes went roving anymore. There weren't enough of them to spare from the Temples . . . and besides, among the younger generations roving was largely seen as old-fashioned.

That was the opinion Rhia had held, anyway, in the years before she uprooted her Temple-bred beliefs, cast off her robes, and fled.

"Anyway, the headman isn't in the village right now. He left last week—he and his husband—for Columb, west of here."

West. Rhia sighed. *Like I haven't come far enough already.*

"If you'd like to leave it with me, I can attest to its safe delivery. I'll give it to him soon as he comes back."

"No—thanks, but I can't. The delivery instructions are clear. Into his hands, no other."

The woman frowned. "Well . . . come into town, then, and we'll put you up somewhere."

Rhia rolled her shoulders under the weight of the pack, feeling weeks of tension threading her muscles tightly together. The attraction of sleeping under a roof warred with her sense of propriety. "I couldn't impose—"

"It's no imposition. It would be for your safety." The acolyte took Rhia's wrist and tugged gently. "I'm Mireille. Come."

Mireille led Rhia into town. The houses were all single-story, wooden construction with shingled roofs and gap-toothed front porches. A small central square was bracketed by larger buildings Mireille identified as they walked: "Headman's house. General store. Bar."

As darkness fell, people threaded across the porches, either going in from a day of work or coming out into the cooler evening air. Lanterns dotted the windows. There was a hum of barely audible conversation. A dry, incessant cough came from inside one of the houses.

Rhia watched the people move, mesmerized by their presence after weeks alone on the road. She expected to field some conversation, because in a town this size any new arrival would generate interest, but no one spoke to her. Cerretour seemed subdued, wrung out.

"No Temple?" she asked, more to break the quiet than out of any real curiosity.

"I'm afraid not," Mireille said. "This far out, they get by with traveling Priests. Someone passes through twice, maybe three times, a year."

They walked through a sea of darkness punctuated by buoys of light from the windows. Rhia noticed there were fewer lights than there were houses.

"Where are all the—" Rhia started to say, but Mireille pointed down the road. A gleam of orange light flickered in the grassland beyond the town.

"That's a group coming off the prairie," she said quietly. "They're on the other side of the spring."

She strode into the darkness. Rhia hesitated, lingering in the cast-off light pooling in the street, but when

Mireille didn't look back, inertia and curiosity pulled her forward.

Beyond the shelter of the houses, a smooth breeze cut across the earth, pulling all the tall grass in one direction. A group of people advanced in from the grasslands, led by an elderly man holding a lantern—the source of the light that had been bobbing across the grass. The group looked footsore and grimy, like they'd been out in the sun all day.

"Good evening Mireille."

"Creff." Mireille stepped forward, her hands folded in the sleeves of her robe. "Did you find anything?"

The lantern-holder shook his head wearily. "Nothing. We're back out tomorrow."

Mireille nodded, an expression of practiced concern on her face. "You're all in my prayers."

From the street behind her, Rhia heard someone break into tears. She turned and saw a woman standing on her porch, face in her hands. A man rubbed her back.

The group continued around the spring and past Rhia and Mireille. Rhia made brief eye contact with a tall bald man, who regarded her with frank curiosity.

"What are they—" Rhia started to ask, but Mireille shook her head. Several other men in the group were staring too. Hostility emanated like heat waves. Belatedly, Rhia realized they were staring at her.

"Not too trusting of strangers around here," Mireille murmured once they were out of earshot.

"They seemed trusting of you," Rhia pointed out.

The other woman flashed a weary smile. "I'm not a stranger anymore."

Rhia watched until the men's slumped shoulders and drooping heads vanished down the road, then turned back to the acolyte. "Mireille, what's going on? Did more people used to live here? Every second house is empty."

Mireille's lips knit together. She gestured at the ground by her feet. "Look at the soil."

They stood at the edge of a long dark arc set into the grass. *They're on the other side of the spring,* Mireille had said, but there was no spring here. No water, even. Rhia didn't need her Talent to tell that. Where there should have been wavering reflections of the stars overhead, maybe a smear of lanternlight blobbing near the shore, the ground was even, velvety darker-on-dark where the grass ended and the earth fell away.

Rhia knelt and touched the dirt. Dry as ash. An investigatory tendril of Talent verified her intuition. There was no aquifer beneath the spring, or if there was, it was empty.

"We've been in drought for weeks now," Mireille said quietly. "The little creeks out on the prairie are running a bit, so that helps, but this spring was one of the main sources of water for the town, and . . . as you see."

Rhia shook her head. "A drought is when there's no rain. This is—"

Desiccated. The springbed was dead, all the liquid sucked out of it. She thought of the hollow-cheeked sky mummies they made from the dead on the southern plateaus. If it was possible, the earth beneath her was drier than the rest of the prairie. It repelled her Talent like a rubber ball bouncing off brick.

She had never felt something like this before, ground so dry it formed a crust against the wetter earth around it. Rhia pressed her palm against the dirt, trying to understand.

"The summer was looking to be dry anyway, but the spring dried up. Then the well ran out two weeks ago and that really sealed it. That's when Micah, the headman, left. They're looking for help, or water if they can find it, but . . ." Mireille's mouth flattened. "It's a challenging time. Columb is the nearest big town, and it's nearly ten leagues from here."

Rhia sat back on her heels.

"That's what those people were doing?" she asked. "The ones coming back from the prairie. Looking for water?"

Mireille offered Rhia a hand up. "No," she said. "Come home with me."

Rhia frowned. There was something else bothering her, something more than could be explained by what Mireille was saying. Disquiet fluttered up from her gut. As they walked away, she looked over her shoulder at the spring. The patch of dark dry earth looked like a fatal wound on the body of the land.

Unnatural.

They walked back together through the ink-dark streets. What few lights had been visible in the houses were rapidly winking out.

Mireille led her up the path to a small house. "This is mine. Let me feed you, and I'll get you settled in one of your own."

Rhia hesitated on the threshold. "You don't have to—"

"I know I don't, but I'd like to nonetheless." Mireille smiled. "Come in. Sit."

Inside, there was a small square table with two chairs, a makeshift kitchen, a tiny altar in one corner of the room. Rhia watched, skittish, as the acolyte knelt in front of the altar, clapped her hands, and rang a bell. The gestures were familiar, but everything else was different, washed in different colors than she was used to. Even the figures of the sovereigns were slightly alien to Rhia's eye; their workmanship cruder than those she'd grown up with. The effigies of Artis, Shirin, Luus, and Enni were barely identifiable by the symbols usually associated with them— book, wave, sword, and scythe.

It all looks homemade. Must be a local tradition.

A puff of incense smoke punched her back in time— frankincense and warm spices, almost exactly the blend of scents that had wafted through her hair and clothing in childhood. She swallowed a noseful of memories and the rock in her throat. The incense made her eight years old again, too short to reach the lanterns hanging from the eaves. It made her Talent part water in a basin for the very first time, drawing a line of clean dry copper across the bottom. It made the silent presence of her brother on her flank, ever beside her as ever they were beside each other.

It was the bright wet eyes of her foster mother Celandine as she turned away from Rhia, face set in denial. It was the rattling slam of the side gate in the white-stone wall on the night she'd run away. It was everything she felt about the Temple: anger and injury and longing all at once.

For a moment the room swam in her vision. As she blinked the water out of her eyes, her gaze fell again on the altar. The largest figure on the altar was a rough representation of Enni, sovereign of the land. The goddess' features were crude and blocky. *Good thing Mireille's an acolyte, because she's not much of a woodworker.*

Mireille bumped the altar as she stood. A ceramic bowl of dried flowers bounced off the table. It paused halfway to the floor, hovering in midair, and the petals spun in a lazy whirlwind above it. The bowl lifted and settled itself back on the table, flowers placing themselves delicately in the basin. Mireille saw Rhia watching her and smiled.

"You're Earth Talented," Rhia observed.

"That I am. Although I'd swap it for a Water Talent right now, if I could."

Rhia's gut twisted. Mireille had no idea that a Water Talent shared the room with her at this moment.

She fought the urge to confess. The impulse to disclose to a Priest, to be helpful by default, was one she had learned in childhood. Even now, leagues away from Roundtree and years away from her Temple cell, the muscle memory was there. The flush of guilt accompanying her decision to keep her mouth shut came from a much younger version of herself. But that guilt was followed just as quickly by a reflexive flinch away from it.

The Temple had raised her and then rejected her. She had left that part of her life in the dust, shed it like snakeskin.

There's no water under the spring. It's not like I can call it out of the air. I can't fix the drought.

Unaware of Rhia's distress, Mireille lit a couple of candles, set a tin plate at the table, laid it with bread and cheese, a cold sausage, some wrinkly grapes. They sat together.

"I'm sorry for how those men looked at you, the ones we passed in the street," Mireille said. "It didn't used to be like that. Folks here are reserved, but they greeted me warmly when I arrived. The drought changed everything."

"What were they doing out on the prairie?" Rhia asked, relieved for the change in topic. "Hunting?"

"They're looking for someone—a young woman who went missing a few weeks back. Tansin. She disappeared out of her bed one night, hasn't been seen since. They've been out there every day."

The prairie was hard country. Unless the girl had run off with a friend or lover, *missing for a few weeks* meant her bones were gleaming white under the moon somewhere. It felt rude to say that out loud, though.

Rhia picked up a grape and squeezed it, felt the juice inside compress under her fingers.

Who can blame them? No one can control a drought. They want to feel like they're doing something. Of course they're spending every day looking for a girl everyone knows is dead or run away.

"No water, someone missing . . . Sounds like they're having a rough go," she offered when Mireille didn't say anything more.

The acolyte nodded. "That's why I'm still here. They recommend you don't stay in one place for too long, when you go roving. I thought I'd leave weeks ago. But the drought . . ." She wrapped her hands around a clay cup half-full of tepid water. The lines of her knuckles were threaded with dirt, her fingernails torn and shaggy. "I'm the only Talent here. I can get their crops to grow, their plants to fruit out of season. It kills the plant, I do it often enough, but it's that or starve. Nothing grows without aid. They need me."

Rhia rolled that around in her mind. "Why don't they all just pack up and leave?"

Mireille looked at her like she'd said something odd. "This is their home. Most people, they haven't been more than a couple miles beyond the farmland. They were born here. Their ancestors are buried here. They'll stay as long as they can."

Rhia tried to put herself in the mind of someone who had never left her hometown, never thrown most of her belongings into a pack and set out with a rough timeline and never-before-seen destination over the horizon, and couldn't. She'd been leaving places for her entire adulthood. The road dust on her boots was thicker than the original leather.

"And now that's Tansin's gone . . ." Mireille continued. "Some of them don't want to leave until she comes home. They've lost a lot. They're clinging to what they have."

"What will you do?" Rhia asked.

The acolyte leveled a flat blue gaze at her. "Until the gods intercede? All I can."

Mireille led Rhia to an unoccupied one-room house. Table, chair, bed, pegs on the wall to hang her clothes, a tiny hearth with years of dust sleeping in it.

"Tomorrow we can see about getting you introduced around," Mireille said as Rhia dropped her pack at the head of the bed and dug through it for her lantern. "People will warm to you more once they recognize you. Everyone loves a Courier, right?"

Rhia snorted. "Only when you're carrying good news."

An animal cried in the grassland outside.

Rhia burst to her feet, dropping the lantern. The sound was so loud and close, it could have been outside the front door.

The call was short and harsh. The hair on Rhia's arms stood up. She had heard plenty of coyotes make their gulping yaps out on the plains, and foxes scream in heat, and even the deep, sonorous bay of wolves once or twice, up in the mountains by Liennis. This wasn't any of those. This gutteral, raw-throated bark shared traits with a human voice.

It sounds like someone who's been screaming for hours, she thought and shivered.

Beside her, Mireille held perfectly still, expression serene, seemingly undisturbed by the noise.

The sound faded.

"What was that?" Rhia whispered when it became apparent that the animal wasn't going to howl again. She felt sweat dotting the small of her back.

Mireille reached down and righted the lantern. She set it neatly on a small end table. "The locals call it the greyhowler."

"What the fuck is a *greyhowler*?" Belatedly it occurred to her that a priest probably wouldn't appreciate profanity, even if she was only a baby priest. ". . . Sorry."

The acolyte smiled thinly. "Don't worry about it."

She fished in an inner pocket in her robes, came up with a length of flint on a cord. Kneeling, she pulled the chimney out of the lantern and struck sparks onto the wick. "It's a local legend. Something like a coyote—but bigger—with long arms and a human face. They say it's afraid of the sunlight; it buries itself in the earth during the day and digs out at night. It eats the dead, and they say if you're alone on the prairie and hear its call, the next person to die will be you."

In the halls of her memory, Rhia's foster mother Celandine folded long-fingered hands over the opening of her priest robes and smiled indulgently. "*Do you want a scary story?*"

Mireille interpreted Rhia's silence as waiting for further explanation and added: "It's not real."

"*That*"—Rhia pointed at the house's one window, at the the night and prairie and wide world beyond—"was real."

"Aye, and whatever it is—a rabid coyote, a feral dog, a plains cat—it sounds big and dangerous. It's been crying outside of town every night. That's why I offered to put you up. It's why no one's going out alone at night right now."

Rhia had never heard a dog or a plains cat make a call that made the hair on the back of her neck stand up, and while she'd never seen a rabid coyote, she suspected it wouldn't sound like that either.

She thought of the last few nights she'd spent on the prairie, warm and restless under the open sky. All the little rustles and snaps in the underbrush as one set of wildlife put itself to bed and another arose. *Ground owls*, she'd thought sleepily. *Mice. Rabbits and groundhogs. Maybe a puma.* She had drifted off making a little inventory of mostly harmless animals, the way a child counts sheep.

Now she imagined something else, a body long and leonine, draped through the compacted earth like an alligator hanging in swamp water. Two acid-yellow eyes blinking open as night fell, peering through the prairie grass an inch off the ground. The sudden, fatal eruption as it attacked.

She shivered.

"How long have you been hearing it?"

"A couple weeks now. I'm sorry I didn't think to warn you—it usually goes off after dark, and we've all just . . . gotten used to it."

Rhia released a puff of nonplussed air. "Gotten used to it!"

"I know." Mireille grimaced. "Between the drought and Tansin going missing, we've had more urgent things to worry about. It hasn't come into town yet. Not that we know of."

"Yeah, well. If that's the sound it makes, I think you'd find out pretty quick."

"Right?" Mireille gave her a rueful smile. "Anyway, I'll leave you to it."

"Are you sure?" Rhia cast another wary eye at the darkness outside the house. "It could be—"

Mireille shook her head. "It's fine. I go out at night all the time. Please, don't be afraid. It's safe in town, I promise."

Rhia was not convinced. "If you say so."

They bid each other good night and Mireille left. Rhia watched until the acolyte's narrow frame disappeared into the gloom and shut the door firmly behind her.

Rhia washed with two palmsful of water from the skin in her pack, pretending her hands weren't shaking. She shoved the pack under the head of the bed, her boots under the foot, and lay down. Habit, to keep all her gear close to hand in the night, but a comforting ritual, too. Tension knitted her shoulder blades together and she tried to exhale it away.

The dark world outside was silent. Too quickly, her imagination filled it; the held breath, the hanging tension of a predator's calculation, the moment's pause between crouch and leap.

She wished there was a lock on the door.

She closed her eyes and dropped a hand down to press against the soft bulge of the waterskin in the pack, listening to the faint slosh. Already comforting, the presence of water, and she'd barely been here for four hours.

She smelled dust and dry thatch.

This place is dying.

The smart thing to do would be to turn around and walk out of this bone-parched town first thing in the morning. But she'd sworn an oath to deliver the parcels entrusted to her, into the hands of their intended recipients and none other. She didn't know what was in the letter in her pack, couldn't weigh its importance against her own ease and safety, but that didn't matter. This was the commitment she'd made: to take things where they were destined to go and deliver them to those waiting. This was her job, and her job was her life.

Mireille's tired hands wrapped around the clay cup flickered across her mind's eye.

The acolyte's determination was relatable; her flat commitment to do *All I can* until circumstances changed. That was Temple-taught, pounded into every acolyte during the hundreds of exercises that prepared them for the Priesthood initiation trials. It had taken as much determination for Rhia to leave the Temple. If she hadn't, she might well be in a position like Mireille's even now, ministering to a flock out in the boondocks, trying to solve problems far in excess of her capabilities. Trying and failing and unable to quit. *Trust the gods and do the work*, is what they told her in the Temple. Rhia knew Mireille would work until she dropped, because that's what Rhia would have done.

Everyone broke eventually. How long would it take before Mireille gave up? Before the town was empty? How many weeks could they survive without even a flutter of rain?

Rhia rolled onto her side, facing the door, knuckles still curled against her pack, and closed her eyes.

This isn't my problem.

She thought of the altar in Mireille's house. Humble, just a spot to kneel in front of and collect your thoughts. The bare minimum to worship with: bell and incense and effigy and imagination. The effigies, hand-made. There was no Temple out here. No Priests. Just one acolyte alone at the edge of the world, trying to keep everyone inside at night. A woman with a job. A girl out on the prairie somewhere, lost or hurt or dead. A wild animal prowling outside. The moment between crouch and leap.

Rhia was falling asleep.

The acolyte and the effigies and the Temple collided in her memory with the imaginary monster outside. The Temple had a monster like that. Celandine had told her about it when she was little.

"The lusus mendace is the guardian of truth-seekers. It walks the earth at night hunting those who tell lies. It smells deceit, and when it smells a lie, it will hunt the liar across the face of the earth."

Was the roof of her mouth dry, or was she just imagining it?

The greyhowler eats the dead. It eats lies. Lies are the corpse of hope, of what we want to be true. The greyhowler and the lusus mendace are the same. All monsters are one monster.

Out on the prairie, a coyote yipped, and then another, and then the night was filled with the sound of coyotes. Definitely coyotes. Those calls, at least, were familiar.

There's no such thing as greyhowlers.

The words in her mind turned into pictures. Dry coughs and dusty tongues in every house in town. Skin crumpling into raisin folds. Rough scaly animal pads stalking silently through every unlocked door, raising tiny puffs of dust, carrying blood in ruddy eyes and splashed across sharp teeth.

She imagined death in sleep, death by dry-throat gasping, until her imagination became dreams.

The morning broke tall-skied and cloudless. Rhia woke when the sun sliced through the window and across her face, grimacing away from it and rolling over into the wall before she remembered where she was.

Cerretour. The letter. The missing girl.

Her throat creaked with dust. She came back to herself.

She checked her pack first thing, more from habit than out of any real paranoia. The letter: tucked into the secret compartment hidden in a seam, right where she'd left it, seals and ribbons undisturbed. Her belongings: just as she'd left them. Her boots: undisturbed under the bed, one of them flopping drunkenly against the other.

Her lips were dry, and from the tightness across her cheeks and nose, she had picked up a bit of a sunburn over the last few days. She pulled a mouthful of water out of her waterskin and swished it around her teeth, tasting sleep and dust. She pulled on her one remaining clean shirt and resolved to figure out how folks around here were cleaning their clothing with such tight water rationing.

She didn't want to waste water on a pot of tea it would soon be too hot to drink. She settled for another swig from the waterskin and went to see what was going on outside.

Seen in full daylight, Cerretour had more charm than had been in evidence last night. Her loaner house stood in a row of similarly-sized houses, and while many appeared to lay empty, she could pick out the occupied ones by their neat yards and laundry lines. Pots of herbs and wilting flowers were protected under shady porches. Someone laughed through an open window. Rhia smelled bread baking. The early summer sun bleached the dust in the road to the color of old bone, and the promise of heat hung in the air, but she could feel the liveliness of the town piercing through it.

A group of children scrambled in the dust, shrieking with laughter. Rhia stood in the doorway, waterskin in one hand, and watched them roll like tumbleweeds up the street. She kept the smile off her face as one of them, then all of them, noticed her and went uniformly silent, staring bug-eyed at her silhouette in the doorway until she twinkled her fingers at them and they tore off.

Cute. If they had heard the howling last night, they were unfazed by it. Even a drought and a wild animal couldn't keep kids from playing together. Rhia didn't really like kids, but even she had to admit that that was kind of nice.

Farther down the street, a small group was assembling near the edge of the prairie. Probably another search party for that missing girl. Rhia remembered the open hostility with which some of the men had stared at her last night and weighed the pros and cons of going to meet them. She had no idea when the headman would be back. However long that took, it would feel *especially* long if people were glaring daggers at her every time she stepped outside.

People will warm to you more once they recognize you, Mireille had said. *Everyone loves a Courier, right?*

Not if you're sticking your nose into their business, Rhia thought. *I should just leave well enough alone.*

On the other hand, I'm one more pair of eyes to search with, and it never hurts to ingratiate yourself to the locals.

On the other other hand, going out on the prairie for the day means that if the headman comes back, I'll miss him until the evening, or maybe even tomorrow.

On the other other other hand, sitting around waiting for something all day is the worst. I'm a Courier, for gods' sakes. Going places is my whole deal.

Underneath the calculations running in her head was the sound of the woman on the porch last night, sobbing into a man's shoulder as the search party trudged empty-handed up the street.No one had missed Rhia when she left the Temple, as far as she was aware. The lack of pursuit or search after she'd run away had sent its own message: She'd been too much trouble. No one had wanted her back.

Here, today, someone wanted Tansin back.

She went back inside to prepare: donning her sun hat, boots, and loose clothes. She pulled the half-full waterskin's strap over her shoulder. As a last step, she took the letter she had carried to Cerretour out of her pack, wrapped it in a kerchief, and tucked it into the waistband of her pants. She wanted to never be separated from her deliveries if she could help it. It was a superstitious ritual, yeah . . . but like all superstitious rituals, not doing it was more stressful than doing it.

The crowd was about twenty people of mixed genders, mostly adults but with a few teenagers. Rhia felt like her clothes were so dirty she was off-gassing a small cloud of dust everywhere she went, but she affixed herself to the back of the group and listened to the person who was speaking.

"Today we'll head into the trees. She mighta shored up there, taken shelter. Look for anything might be a sign she's been through. Don't call out for her; listen instead. If she's hurt, she may not be able to make much noise."

"What's *she* doing here?" someone cut in, their voice clearly directed at Rhia.

Every eye in the group fell on her. She held herself tall, tried not to think about the sweat stains under her armpits. She noted with some relief that she was dressed in much the same fashion as the other searchers. Dirtiest, by far, but at least she didn't look unprepared.

"Mireille told me someone was missing," she said. "I want to help look."

"Who are you, stranger?" an older man with a softly lined face asked her. Rhia recognized him as the man who'd been carrying the lantern at the head of the group that came in from the prairie last night.

"Rhia Silver. I'm a Courier. I have a delivery for your headman, but since he's not here . . . " She spread her hands. "Figured I could be useful."

"This is a town concern," a woman said brusquely. "We don't need no help from someone don't even know us."

"No, you don't." Rhia kept her voice quiet enough to lean people toward her so they could hear. It was a trick she'd figured out after a few different encounters with crowds of strangers; low volume drew people's ears, made them focus on hearing her, but also kept her harmless-looking. "But more eyes can't hurt. I won't hold you back. I can track and read a trail as well as anyone. I made it all the way out here from Tellemont on what I could trap and gather."

The crowd took that in.

A bird whistled out in the grass.

"Besides . . . " Rhia rocked from her heels to the balls of her feet and back again. "I really hate sitting around."

"Don't we all," someone murmured, and someone else chuckled.

"I don't think—" the woman started indignantly.

"Leave it, Joyen." The older man put up a stilling hand. "It's as she says. No harm in one more. Now listen up: once we're past the treeline, don't get separated."

"Else the *greyhowler* gets you," someone muttered, speaking the creature's name with exaggerated fear. Someone else giggled.

The man shot an irritated look in the direction of the voices. "Walk in a line, try not to get too far ahead or behind anyone. Anyone finds anything, the whole line stops. Got me?"

They got him. The group headed for the far edge of town, Rhia included.

The search party set out, heading through town to the sparse gatherings of trees that stood on the far side of the buildings. Rhia looked down a side street out of idle curiosity and spotted Mireille, her hands spread wide over some kids' heads, probably the same group that had bumbled past Rhia's door that morning. The breeze was in the wrong direction for Rhia to hear what she was saying to them, but from the expression on her face, she was having fun. The children were laughing, frisking under her arms and around her robe like rabbits.

"That girl's a real blessing," the older man observed. He'd fallen into stride with Rhia so quietly she almost hadn't noticed him.

"She's not a girl," Rhia said with the reflex of someone who'd been *girl*ed one too many times in the course of her work. "She's a grown-ass woman with a grown-ass job."

"Easy now, no offense intended. When you hit my age, suddenly everyone's impossibly young. I call my own son a boy, and he's pushing fifty." When he smiled, the man's eyes nearly disappeared in a collapse of wrinkles. "I'm Creff. Tansin's my niece. Rhia, was it?"

"Yeah." She was still prickly about girl, but part of this whole excursion was to build positive relationships, so when he extended his hand, she took it. He was so calloused it was like taking a hand-shaped block of wood. "Rhia Silver."

Mireille had caught sight of Rhia and was waving. She and Creff waved back. As they continued past the street, the acolyte turned her attention to shepherding the children in one direction, a warm, tolerant look on her face.

Rhia thought of her own childhood in the Temple, the unquestioning obedience with which she had followed Celandine, and suppressed a shudder.

"No question about who's doing work," Creff continued as they walked by. "When she's not growing plants, she's minding the kids so their parents can get planting done, search for water, or go looking for Tansin. Holds services for us every day, alternating dawn on one day and sundown the next, so everyone who wants to can join. Working herself to the bone, that one, and for us who're next to strangers."

"That's nice," Rhia said automatically, trying to shake off her discomfort. "She sounds really disciplined. What Temple did she come from?"

"Ah, I couldn't say. She showed up about six weeks ago, and thank gods she did—Tansin went missing not long after, and then the well dried up . . . It's been a hard patch. She's really held the town together, especially since Micah left. Folk rely on her."

"Micah—the headman?"

"Aye. And my vow-son. He's wed to that fifty-year-old boy I was talking about."

"How long have you been doing"—the jerk of her chin encompassed the search party, the missing woman, the hushed blonde prairie beyond—"this?"

"Oh, weeks now." He winked at her. "See, I hate sitting around too."

Rhia cracked a smile in spite of herself.

"Real shame, the circumstances, though. Tansin couldn't have gone missing at a worse time."

"Why's that?"

"She was Talented—*is*, I should say, excuse me." He tapped both shoulders in an unfamiliar pattern that was clearly intended to ward off bad luck.

The search party passed beyond the last buildings and moved out onto the open prairie. The road lay to the south, and a wide, well-trod path jutted off it and led east. The large outbuilding that Mireille had come from last night stood alone at the end of the path, set away from both the trees and the houses in town. It was dark daub with a sturdy roof, one door, and no windows. Rhia figured it for some kind of storage building. Maybe it had seen more use in more prosperous times, but right now, it looked abandoned.

The dirt was scuffed in swooping arcs along the path, evidence of regular traffic headed in that direction, but she didn't see anyone walking along it now. What reason would anyone have to visit an abandoned building? It was hard for Rhia to imagine anyone traveling out beyond the shelter of the streets with some wild creature howling on the prairie every night.

Maybe there wasn't a creature at all. Maybe it was just a prankster, a kid getting up to mischief.

"The one Talent in the whole town," Creff said quietly, more to himself than to her. "Our little wellspring."

Rhia pulled her attention back to the conversation. "Tansin was a Water Talent?"

"Aye, albeit a real soft one." He didn't seem to notice her distraction. "Probably only second or third degree. It's a shame, the thing the girl wanted most in the world was to be a Priest, but she wouldn't've come near passing the tests. Woulda been more of a blessing her staying right here as our dowsing-witch. There's lotsa different ways to serve the gods, we told her. Tried to, any rate. She wouldn't hear it, though. Wanted more'n anything to go to a big city, find a real Temple, get herself trained and do the trials and all of it.

"Don't know why you'd travel leagues to get told what's plain as the nose on your face to everyone around you, but people can be funny like that, can't they? You tell a person they can't have what they want, just makes 'em want it more."

The outbuilding was shrinking behind them, the trees growing ahead. Rhia tried to refocus. "So you think she ran away. Not a wild animal or that . . . whatever they're saying is your local monster."

"The greyhowler? Saints and sovereigns, no. That's something altogether else."

"Wait, you really believe in it?" Incredulity made her tone extremely rude. "Sorry. I'm just—surprised. It sounds like . . ." *Superstitious nonsense. A fable. A folktale told to children.* ". . . It sounds like no one's seen it," she finished weakly.

His bushy white eyebrows chased wrinkles up his forehead on their way to his hairline. "Don't see as how that's relevant. I ain't never seen the capital neither, but people tell me it's there."

"I mean . . . Every town's got a monster or a boogeyman or a ghost, right?" Rhia tried to figure out how to express her skepticism without offending the man. "We used to have a monster like that in the—where I'm from, in south Artesia. It was called the lusus mendace, it hunted people who told lies . . . It's made up, though. We used to scare children with it. No one really believed in it."

Creff shrugged. "Story like that's fine for foreigners, miss, begging your pardon. Out here, we don't gotta believe in the greyhowler. It surely believes in us."

Rhia shook her head, but Creff just kept walking.

Unbidden, the image of a long, knobby limb tipped in coal-colored claws emerging from the grass injected itself into her mind's eye. She saw herself, suddenly, from the imagined perspective of a beast. Whisks of tall grass obscured her view of the long-legged woman in the sun hat who lingered a moment too long behind the group, the plants parting silently as she crept closer—

The search party had moved on without Rhia. She told herself it was just pent-up energy that made her trot through the grass to rejoin them. The skin between her shoulderblades prickled and she scolded herself for scaring herself with nothing, like a child laying in bed afraid of things imagined in the dark. *Don't be stupid. The lusus mendace is make-believe. One old guy believing in greyhowlers doesn't mean there is such a thing. Are such things. Whatever.*

Besides, Mireille said it only comes out at night.

The search party approached the line of trees abutting the northern edge of town. The warm wind off the prairie played with the tip of Rhia's braid, plucked it over her shoulder. The hip-high grass brushed her fingertips with tickling kisses. Her gaze skimmed across the rippling patterns, looking for breaks in the motion—stillness or spots where the wind's rhythm was interrupted, indicating that something was laying in wait or moving through the grass.

This close to the copse, she could see that it was actually . . . well, she was from Roundtree and would never call this meager collection of sticks and rubbly earth a *forest*, but it was more trees than she'd expected. The trees were stunted, stooped toward the earth as if proximity would bring water up to their crowns faster. They had shaggy bark and knobby, lobed leaves. There was enough of them that it was hard to see more than a few yards beyond where they stood.

The group stopped outside the treeline, arraying itself in a loose line. Rhia found herself between Creff and a tall dark-haired teenager, about twenty feet of open space on either side. The line advanced at a gentle stroll, falling silent as they crossed into the shadows of the trees.

The break from sunlight was welcome. Rhia breathed in a lungful of shade-scented air, dry earth, dusty bark, mast. Small bushes clustered between the tree trunks. The trees closed around them. Sunlight slanted through the leaves. The group slowed to a halting walk, examining the ground a foot at a time.

Her Talent flickered in acknowledgement of the water sliding through each tree, the faint trickles of moisture that fed the deep-gripping roots underground. There was water here, as she'd expected, given the presence of larger plants and trees . . . but not enough to make a dent in the drought. It was like the speckles of rainwater that would make your fingers squeak on glass, when what they needed was a monsoon.

A branch snapped to her right and she jumped. The dark-haired teenager had tripped on something, was righting himself on the trunk of a tree. When he caught Rhia looking at him, he blushed and glared at the ground. Rhia vaguely remembered the awkward, coltish phase of adolescence where her feet seemed to be two different sizes all the time and her limbs a half-inch longer with every stretch. She pretended to study the bark of a nearby tree.

The underbrush wasn't hard to read. Rhia saw traces of small animal life: pebbles of rabbit shit, tufts of fur tangled in loose leaves, an owl pellet, a puff of pinfeathers that was all that remained of an unlucky bird. She looked for anything out of place: loose threads in unusual colors, impressions in the brush where something larger than a deer might have curled up to hide or sleep, the distinctive signs of bipedal motion across the ground.

And saw nothing. If Tansin had come through this area, it hadn't been near here.

After an hour of silence, her interest in the search withered. She grew irritable, then bored. Her mind wandered. Again, she saw Mireille's parchment-dry hands clenched around the clay cup of water.

The ceramic bowl drifted upward through the air, guided by the invisible hand of the acolyte's Earth Talent.

I'd swap it for a Water Talent right now, if I could.
What will you do?
Until the gods intercede? All I can.

It was such an automatic answer. Rhia had had those reflexes once, the ones that put the words in your mouth before you even thought them. Trust the gods and do the work. To be righteous is to safeguard those around you. She had recited the Shepherd's Prayer every evening, along with all the other Talented children in the foster house. It was utterly unsurprising to find another Temple-raised woman here in the heart of a desiccated plain, trying to keep together as many bodies and souls as she could, even if her Talent wasn't suited for it. Even if it would ultimately prove impossible. Rhia hoped the headman would come back, or the drought would break, or something—anything—would change before Mireille overextended herself to an unrecoverable degree.

That was the thing about the Temple. They trained you to give of yourself *selflessly*, as if it was even possible to deny the self when giving from it, to turn yourself inside out like an emptying waterskin. Every year, acolytes died attempting the initiation trials of Priesthood. The Temple revered them as martyrs and painted their faces on the walls of the trial chambers. Until the next year, when the vernal equinox came and they painted the walls white. Blank canvases awaiting new faces.

That was one of the things Rhia had thrown in her brother's face the night she left the Temple. That all they were learning in the Temple was how to be grain, and if they survived being grain, how to be a millstone.

And if you needed anything from the Temple beyond a sweep of the scythe or water over the wheel, they turned you away. Rhia had learned this lesson hard and fully, and the taste of it still burned in her mouth, pepper-hot.

Water flared, simultaneously bright and loud in her mind's eye, startling her out of her thoughts. It was nearby, within paces, running, and aboveground.

She probably made too much noise breaking through the underbrush, but she didn't care. She hadn't seen running water in days, and knowing it was out there was both a balm and a goad. Someone called out behind her, but she ignored them.

The trees broke as quickly as they'd swallowed her, and a wide swath of burnished prairie opened ahead of her. Running along the verge of the grass, a narrow creek bubbled and spat. All too quickly it disappeared among the tree roots.

Kneeling beside it, Rhia plunged her hands in and then scrubbed her face. The water was cool, and immersing her hands in it was invigorating. Suddenly every inch of unwashed skin was apparent to her. She tipped a palmful on her head, hissing through her teeth at the chill.

Rhia pulled her waterskin down off her shoulder and eased the mouthpiece into the flow. The average person probably shouldn't fill a waterskin from an unknown source, but a Water Talent never had to worry about dirt or illnesses when she drew water from the earth.

"Good find, Courier." Creff was close behind. "I thought we'd mapped all the ground-running streams around town, but this is new."

"How'd you spot it?" The dark-haired teenage boy knelt next to her. The sight of the water stretched his eyes as big as goose eggs.

"Sharp ears," Rhia lied. "I heard something different from the tree noise, that's all." The last thing she wanted right now was to field a bunch of questions about being Talented.

"Well, we'll send some lads out tomorrow with buckets, see what we can bring back. It won't water the crops, but we'll get some washing done, at any rate." Creff nodded with satisfaction.

"What's that?"

Rhia followed the teenage boy's pointing finger to the other side of the creek. Her eyes glossed over it at first, but she looked until a change in shape snapped into focus.

About four paces past the creek, the grass curved in a shallow arc, flattened and bent into a tidy bower. Something, or someone, had rested here, and recently enough that the grass hadn't sprung back into shape.

"She was here," the young man breathed. Hope drew his body into electric lines, his entire posture focused on the depression in the grass. "Tansin was *here*."

"Now, Rensoa, could be anything made that mark," Creff said. "Deer or a wildcat or—"

"You think it's the greyhowler," Rensoa scoffed.

"I said it could be anything."

Rhia stood and stepped carefully over the creek, approaching the scoop-shaped depression in the grass. Creff said something cautionary behind her, but she ignored him. The prairie breeze pushed past her, carrying the other voices away with it. If she hadn't known the pair were behind her, she could have thought herself the only person out here on the edge of the lonesome country.

The wind whispered, tugging the tips of the grass along with it. Rhia skated her palms over the tops of the grass as she moved carefully around the perimeter of the depression, scanning for signs; threads from clothing, the listless stir of hair given false life by the breeze, the cramped claw of a dried hand, the knobby curves of scapulae or spine.

Then, barely visible: a print scraped into the dry earth.

Rhia knelt and stared hard, trying to resolve the shape into something she recognized. It *might* have been a handprint. There were lines from four splayed appendages tracing off it, blurred by speed and grass. Fingers?

The deepest part of the print was the . . . was it the palm of a hand? Or something else? Rhia wavered, arguing with herself. She couldn't be positive that the print was human.

But if it wasn't human, what was it? This was no chubby catprint, nor a dog's dependable square pads or a fox's dainty nails. This was from no animal she'd seen before.

Pressed into the earth at the tip of the shortest appendage, Rhia noted a tiny, arced impression, deeper at one point. A fingernail?

Or a claw.

She sat back all in a rush.

"What'd you find, Courier?" Creff called from the other side of the creek.

Rhia pulled her eyes off the print and scoured the prairie grass for movement. Nothing. Just the wind, the gentle combing motion from horizon to horizon, the towering speedwell sky.

"Not sure," she said. "There's a print over here. But I—"

"Let me see it!" Rensoa charged over the creek and across the curled scoop of grass, kicking through its smooth organic shape and ruining the half-baked hope Rhia had had of combing through it to see if she could determine the direction in which its occupant had departed.

"Watch it," she snapped in a tone that channeled all the exasperated Priests of her childhood and stopped Rensoa so fast he rocked forward on his toes, wincing.

"Sorry." He leaned over hard, staring at the shape pressed into the earth. "That it?"

"That's it." She arched her back, stretching the lower joints in her spine. Something popped.

"Creff?" Rensoa shot a look over his shoulder. "Can you look?"

The elderly man crossed the creek with a muttered complaint and trundled over to their position, a hitch in his step.

The three of them formed a roughly equal triangle around the print. The grass hissed to itself. Rhia hiked the waterskin higher on her shoulder.

"Couldn't say," Creff finally said, but the look he shot Rhia said he was thinking about their earlier conversation. "Might be a cougar. Might not."

"It's not the . . . " The bulge in the boy's throat bobbed from chin to clavicle and back. "It ain't real."

Rhia opened her mouth to say *Of course it's not*, and closed it. The greyhowler wasn't real . . . but she had no idea what had made this print.

"The wild world has room for all manner of things," Creff said softly, almost to himself. He scrubbed a hand over the white stubble on his chin, coming to a conclusion. "Let's get the others over here. See what they have to say."

The search party clustered around the creek, the shaggy remnants of the hollow in the grass, the print. Within moments, there was a circle of flattened grass and drifting dust twenty feet in diameter. Rhia stood at the center of it, one boot on either side of the print, nervous that someone would step on it, feeling weirdly protective.

No one in the search party could identify the print, either. One woman suggested it looked a bit like a child's handprint, and about half the group muttered slow agreement. The other half kept their eyes on the horizon, scanning the grasslands in much the same way Rhia had on the walk to the trees. Looking for motion, looking for its absence.

Eventually— at Rhia's prodding—they fanned out from the creek, scouring the prairie beyond the trees until they'd sweated through their clothes and the sun tipped low in the sky. No one found anything: no more prints, no body, no signs of human life, no Tansin.

"This is useless," a man said near the end of the day. "Every day we've been coming out here, and nothing. She's gone."

Rhia had sat down by the print about twenty minutes ago, and now she picked herself up from the grass, dusting off her knees. Her low back ached from stooping over all day, and she was hungry. She was ready to head back, and from the look of it, the others felt the same. The majority of the search party was already drifting toward the trees and Cerretour beyond them. The breeze coming off the prairie was turning cool. Evening was coming, and with it a wan, tinny cast to the light.

"We can go farther," Rensoa was saying.

"Let's call it for today, Ren," Creff said.

"Just another hour," Rensoa said. "She could be close."

"She's not, son. If she were, don't you think we'd have—heard her?"

Rhia filled in the skip in the man's voice with *found her body.*

"We can't give up now," Rensoa insisted. His cheeks darkened. He gestured toward the hollow where they'd found the scoop of flattened grass. "This is the best sign we've had. She could *be* here."

"Best to get back to town before it's full dark," Creff said. The twisting breeze pulled the vowels out of his mouth, distorted his words. "Let's leave the question of coming out again for tomorrow, when we're all less tired."

Rensoa wheeled, sneered at him. "You're just afraid of the *greyhowler.*" His tone turned the name into an epithet. "The greyhowler isn't *real.*"

"Come now," Creff said. "No need for that."

He stepped up beside Rensoa. Their heads bent together. Rhia shifted from one foot to another, uncomfortable from the proximity to what was clearly a gentle scolding. When the older man pulled back, the teenager's shoulders drooped. When the group turned to return to Cerretour, he lingered behind. Eventually, he drifted along reluctantly, bobbing behind them like a small boat tethered to one larger.

"Do you think you'll come out again tomorrow?" Rhia asked Creff.

He shrugged. "I'd like to, but . . ." His expression filled in the things he didn't want to say. "Folks grow weary of it. Every day she's gone, it seems . . ."

More likely she won't be back.

"You think she's alive," Rhia said.

Creff gave her a sad, tired smile. "Hope is free, Courier."

Rhia wasn't sure what was worse: no one searching for a runaway, like no one had searched for her . . . or everyone searching, only it was too late.

Their shadows stretched out long behind them as the sun brushed the horizon. They passed the road leading to the lone dark outbuilding she'd noted on her way out of town.

"What is that?" she asked, trying to change the subject.

Creff barely looked in the direction she indicated. "Oh, that's the well-house. Used to be where we drew our water from, but as you can see, it's stood empty these last few weeks."

"Then those are . . ." She jerked her chin at a cluster of three similarly-constructed outbuildings on the edge of a weedy field.

"Potting sheds. Mostly we use them for sprouting plants, now. Barely anything's growing out of the earth anymore."

Rhia nodded. "Mireille said something about growing the plants for you."

"Aye, she's a real help with that." A smile brightened the old man's weary face. "Won't get us through till harvest, but there's vegetables for now, thanks to her." His looked over his shoulder at the teenager skulking along the road behind them. "That's something to be grateful for, at any rate."

The search party broke apart into small groups, each heading down their own streets. Rhia and Creff stopped in the middle of the road and watched.

Another ruddy evening painted its light across the houses and down the streets. The town looked like someone had spilled a vat of deep amber honey over its face. Twilight unspooled a skein of lavender across the sky. Creff made an appreciative sound.

Rhia tucked her thumb under the strap on her water-skin, hefted the weight of it into her hand. Thanks to the spring, it was heavier now than it had been this morning. She could imagine what it would be like to live here in the bountiful days, when the prairie bloomed with wildflowers and the water ran cool and clear. She could almost see why someone would want to stay.

They stood together in silence for a time, until they were alone in the road.

"What will you do when you run out of food?" Rhia asked.

"We hope not to," Creff said quietly. "But after that, who's to say. Some folk will leave, for certain. But some will stay."

"This is your home," she said, remembering Mireille last night, insisting the same.

"Aye." He smiled at her. His eyes vanished in shadow as the light bled out of the day. "You see the heart of it."

Rhia shook her head, about to ask what the ones who stayed planned to do, starve to death or die of thirst, but the sound of singing stopped her. The tune was one she knew.

"What is—"

"It's sundown." Creff started down the street, beckoning her beside him. "Come and see."

They didn't walk far—down the block and between two houses. Mireille was at the head of a small group of people standing together on the edge of the prairie, leading them in song. It was a hymn Rhia knew well; she'd sung it herself every year at harvest time from when she was old enough to stand until the year she'd left. Mireille and the singers were giving thanks to the sovereigns for the fruits of the land. That felt a little ironic to Rhia, given the circumstances, but nevertheless, the sound brought a lump to her throat. Even standing too far away to make out individual words, between the tune and her own timeworn memories, she could figure it out. Another couple choruses and a verse and the song would be over.

"Are you faithful, Courier?" Creff asked.

Rhia didn't trust her voice, so she shook her head.

"Ah, a pity. Maybe this won't interest you t'all, then. But it's a comfort to me, and to many of us. The days are uncertain. It's good to feel the presence of the gods."

Rhia felt the presence of her memories and not much else.

Creff trundled forward, attached himself to the back of the small gathering. Rhia heard his careworn, creaking voice lift to join the others. Mireille gave him a welcoming smile, seamlessly conducting the congregation.

Rhia lingered back, forgotten. A cool breeze arced in from the prairie and cut along her shoulders, especially chilly against her sweaty skin. She wished for a robe like Mireille's.

At the time, leaving the Temple had felt like something she was forced into. She had taken their rejection and spun it around, turned it into her own repudiation of them, refusing all contact from her foster mother and the other Priests for years. She had learned to be alone—no hymns, no communal meals, no shared work in the orchards or the records-houses. Every skill she'd learned in the Temple, abandoned. All her prayers, made in silence.

Her emotions now were cool enough she could acknowledge that repudiating the Temple also meant relinquishing things she would never get back.

The group of worshippers swayed together in a fluid motion, one body with many heads and hands. Rhia remembered that feeling, the sense of being caught up and buoyed by the presence of others, the universal self bestowed by being part of a community. Her body drifted into the rhythm, which she halted as soon as she noticed it.

Mireille raised her hands, bringing the song to a close, and a curtain of silence dropped over the crowd.

Rhia walked away. She paced down the empty streets through blood-colored light. She was heading out of town, she realized, back in the direction of the road that had brought her into Cerretour.

The dry spring was just on the edge of town. She paced up to the edge of it and stopped. More of it was visible than last night. The low red light turned the dry earth black, a convincing emulation of the rich dark soil she'd expect to see at the bottom of a pond. She even knelt and drifted her fingers across it, picked up a handful and ground it between her thumb and first two fingers. She was half-hopeful . . . but the earth was dry, dry as bone, dry as ash.

Rhia took a long breath and let the dirt spill through her fingers. Her eyes drifted shut. Moments passed, blurred together into one long instant. She let her mind go. The congregation was far behind her. She was as empty as the spring.

"What are you doing?"

Rhia startled. Mireille had come up behind her as silently as a ghost.

"Nothing," she said, standing. She felt sheepish. "Well. I guess I was checking whether the water was back."

The acolyte nodded with a small sad smile. "I understand the impulse. How was the search today? Did you find anything?"

Different words were on the tip of her tongue: *Useless. Fruitless. Pointless.* Instead, she settled on "No."

"It was kind of you to do," Mireille said. "Joining them. I'm sure they appreciated it."

"Creff did, I think."

"He's such a sweet man."

Mireille stepped up next to Rhia, hands folded in the sleeves of her robe. A cool breeze traced itself in bending grass across the surface of the prairie, briefly invisible as it passed over the empty spring and was felt on the skin. The air smelled like dust and the sweet, heavy scent of drying grass.

"I saw you watching the services," Mireille said after a long moment of silence. "You would have been welcome to join, you know. I know the locals can be withdrawn, but we're all siblings in faith."

Rhia's stomach twisted. She shook her head. "That's not a good idea for me."

"Do you not know the hymns? Don't be embarrassed; half the town didn't know them until after I got here—"

"It's not that." She didn't know what words to use. There was a lump in her throat.

"Are you all right?" Mireille heard the change in her voice, reached up to touch her arm.

Rhia identified the emotion she was having as a fucked-up kind of homesickness, and as soon as she did, recoiled.

"What do you care?" she exclaimed, jerking her arm away from Mireille's hand. "Just because I'm not out singing stupid hymns like a kid in a choir—"

Her voice bounced off the dry bowl of the spring and ricocheted through her ears.

The acolyte took a step back, startled. "I'm sorry, I—"

Rhia snapped her mouth shut, shocked by her own reaction. "No, I'm sorry. I just—that wasn't your fault. I don't—I'm not faithful anymore."

"Anymore?"

"Yeah, I—" Her voice caught and she cleared her throat, trying to regain her composure. "I was raised in the Temple, but I left years ago. It was . . . hard. I don't look back at that part of my life very often, and seeing the congregation tonight made me . . . It was hard."

"I see." Mireille appraised her with a Priest's diagnostic gaze. "From birth?"

"Far as I know, yeah."

"You're an orphan."

"I guess."

"I could see how the Temple could be a difficult place to grow up." Mireille's voice was carefully neutral.

Rhia laughed darkly. "Yeah, you don't know the half of it. It's fine when you're little, but once you're a teenager . . ." She stopped, trying not to let memories engulf her. *Change the subject, don't talk about yourself.* "Do you know what they do to cultivate weak Talents? They call it tempering, and—"

"Please," Mireille interrupted. "I've heard the stories. But they're apocryphal. Tempering is a practice from the old days. They don't do it anymore. I should know, my Talent isn't particularly strong. No one locked me in a box or wrapped me in ice water blankets or . . . well. Tempering doesn't happen anymore."

"Yeah, I know," Rhia shook her head. "But the thought process is still there. They still treat you like you're a thing, a doll or a machine they put food into and get work out of. And if you're Talented—" She stopped, not wanting to give too much of herself away.

Evening dropped a silk shawl over the prairie and the dry spring. The light waned into an uncertain dusty indigo. A bird called in the brush. Rhia shifted from one foot to another, heartsore and embarrassed. She was certain she'd hurt the acolyte's feelings, and none of this was Mireille's fault.

"You're not the only person who's had bad experiences with the Temple, you know," Mireille said quietly, to Rhia's surprise.

"That's not what I'd expect a Priest to say."

"Yeah, well, I'm not a Priest," Mireille said. "I'm an acolyte."

In the heartbeat between Rhia's past receding and Mireille's future arriving, they smiled at each other.

"Creff told me something today," Rhia said. "While we were searching. He said Tansin was Talented. He said she wanted to be a Priest."

Mireille ducked her head and scuffed her toe in the dust. "Did she? I barely spoke to her before she went missing."

The acolyte's response was far away and quiet, disengaged. She could have been remarking on the weather. Rhia couldn't see her facial expression, but there was something in the other woman's voice that made her press the topic: "Do you think she could have run away because of it? Tried to find a Temple where they would train her?"

"Who can say?"

Rhia looked out over the empty spring, through the bronzing prairie grasses and the dust meeting twilight against the horizon.

"I don't know. I think she's dead, Mireille. She couldn't survive out there for long."

Mireille crossed her arms against the evening chill. "Believing she's alive . . . it helps everyone. The scriptures say hope is the only burden that lightens the heart."

"Creff said the wild world had room for everything, or something like that. That anything was possible."

"Just so."

Rhia kicked at the spring's scabby shore. A crust of dry earth broke off and tumbled into the basin, starting a tiny avalanche.

"Mireille, you shouldn't stay."

"Hmm? Why?"

"Look at this." Rhia gestured over the spring. "The drought will kill everything here. Tansin's gone. Creff told me you were growing plants for them and . . . it's not going to be enough. It's not worth it."

"What are you worried about?"

"That you're going to burn your Talent out trying to feed way more people than you can grow for. That you're going to kill yourself trying. The Temple isn't going to care, Mireille. People like—" *Us*, she almost said. "People are disposable to them."

"You don't understand," Mireille said firmly. "If that happens, I'll have given my life to help people. Not the Temple. *People*. That's what a Priest is supposed to do."

"Yeah, well." Rhia shook her head. "You just said you aren't a Priest."

She could barely see Mireille's smile in the gathering dark.

"Have a little faith, Rhia. Everything will work out the way it's supposed to."

It was full dark when she returned to the little borrowed house. After saying goodnight to Mireille, she scurried up the quiet streets, not wanting to draw attention. She tried not to think about a wild animal stalking the perimeter of the town until she was within five paces of her own front door.

The door swung open when she put her hand on the knob.

Weird. It must not have latched properly.

The inside of the house was very dark. She stumbled on something between the bed and the door and caught herself on the small table. The lantern chimney rattled in its housing.

Did I leave something on the floor?

The lantern's tin rim caught a spot of light from the window. There was oil spilled on the outside of it. She wiped the excess off. It took her a moment to find the firestriker—it was on the table where she'd left it the night before, but hidden under a pile of blankets from the bed.

That's not right. She had a clear memory of making the bed before the left that morning.

She lit the lantern and surveyed the room in its honeyed yellow light.

The contents of her pack were upended across the floor and bed, a frozen shout of scattered possessions dotted with scraps of pale white.

She did a fast visual assessment: the tangle of pantlegs and shirts like a floppy, oversize tumbleweed. Planks of jerky and fruit bars and cloth bundles of dried noodles dotting the floor. The blankets in her bedroll, thrown over the little table. The pack itself, empty and sagged in a corner. Scattered over all of it, loose sheets of paper curled restlessly against the breeze from the door— the book she'd been reading on the road, she realized. Someone had torn out its guts.

Tears sprung to her eyes, were as quickly dashed aside. That book had been her companion for the entire walk out here, and she felt its loss like she would a fellow traveler. She'd finished it twice and had been halfway through a third read when she arrived at Cerretour. Why would someone tear up her book?

She started with what was closest—the snarl of dirty clothing that had come out of the bottom of her pack. The pants pockets were turned out.

Someone hadn't just trashed her stuff—they'd rifled through it. Looking for something.

She stood up in a rush and, working methodically across the floor, did a quick and thorough inventory of her belongings.

Nothing was missing. Her clothing, her camping gear, her blankets, everything was here, down to the last dirty sock and sturdy metal pen. Even her money chain, every sliver and quarter and circlet clinking against each other, all accounted for.

She peeled a torn page off the floor. They had torn the book apart looking for something, something that could plausibly be hidden in a book.

Something like a letter.

Rhia touched her belly, felt the reassuring crackle of paper against her fingers. The letter she'd come to Cerretour to deliver was still tucked in the waistband of her pants, right where she'd put it this morning. Someone other than the headman was interested in her delivery.

Something coughed wetly in the street outside.

She'd left the door open.

Rhia turned.

The air outside the house was the deep bruise-color of full darkness. Her eyes had adjusted to the lantern-light and she couldn't make out any detail beyond the rhombus of light spilling through the doorway. Gods knew she'd had hundreds of encounters with animals on the road, whether they were crossing her path or lurking just beyond the light of her campfire. Surely that's all this was. But it was the ragged end of a long day, and she spooked more easily than normal. She knew this and was annoyed by it, but couldn't do anything to prevent it.

"H-Hello?" The catch in her voice infuriated her. She bit her lower lip and rode a wave of bravado.

"You didn't get anything," she said to whatever was out in the darkness. "You should have tried harder."

In the moment, she didn't know if she was talking to whoever had failed to steal the letter, or to the fear that was ricocheting around the inside of her chest. She was sick of it, suddenly, of the imaginary monster and the missing woman and the absent headman and this stupid little dry-ass town in the middle of nowhere.

Two yellow dots blinked out of the darkness. Eyes.

They were too near the ground to be human. Rhia flinched back on instinct. The cough came again, and with it, a wash of scent borne on a cool night breeze: red, raw meat, the acidic funk of predator shit, blood.

Rhia knew she should step back and close the door—put something between her and whatever was out there. Mireille was right, it was something huge—a plains cat or a wolf or, or . . .

Do you want a scary story?

It eats the dead. It eats lies. Lies are the corpse of hope, of what we want to be true.

The wild world has room for all manner of things.

The eyes blinked away and were gone.

Something scuffled across the dirt in the road.

Rhia skittered backward, tripped on a pair of trousers crumpled on the floor, and slammed down on her butt. She was paralyzed, eyes glued to the rectangle of unyielding darkness that yawned through the doorframe. Her mouth was dry. Her palms trembled against the ground.

She would be much easier to pounce on while she was on the floor.

That thought alone got her up and on her feet. She stared into the darkness, waiting.

A sail-eared coyote trotted into the lantern light spilling through the open door. Its coat was mottled grey and tawny, its mouth split long and greedy with thirst.

Its yellow gaze met Rhia's, and it spun and sprinted out of sight. The pad of its paws departing fell silent almost as soon as it was gone. The warm night went quiet and still.

A tense breath rattled out of her, halfway to a laugh.

The wild world has room for all manner of things, including coyotes. Gods above, Rhia. Get it together.

She picked herself up, stepped through the last of her fear, and shut the door hard.

છ

Early the next morning, Rhia found Mireille in a shed on the edge of the farm fields, making plants grow. It was barely past dawn; the tight dryness in the air promised another searing day.

Rhia was blurry-eyed and sore. She had slept badly, startling awake every few hours when she heard things moving in the prairie outside. Near dawn, she heard the rasping cry of the animal they called the greyhowler out in the dark, after which she had given up on sleep altogether. She stayed in the house until the sun was up, organizing her scattered belongings. To pass the time until others were awake, she told herself, but in reality she didn't want to walk the streets without being able to see to the ends of them, especially the ones that let out onto the farmland and prairie.

The sealed letter rested against her abdomen inside the waistband of her pants.

Rhia let herself into the shed as discreetly as she could, trying not to let the door squeak and distract Mireille from her work. The shed's dark interior was a relief, even this early in the day, but the air was dusty and close. She pressed her back against the wall, crossed her arms, and waited.

The acolyte was in a crouch, hands dug into the dark earth in an unfired pot. Moss-colored light leaked from the soil caked around her fingers. Two men, suntanned and ropey with old muscle, looked on in awe as the soil squirmed and bulged. A loop of leaves and vines uncurled from beneath Mireille's hands. Even after their conversation last night, and her awareness of how futile the effort would be to fill dozens of empty stomachs in Cerretour, Rhia marveled to see the Earth Talent at work.

Rhia had seen more devotions than she could remember—from every variety of Talent—but watching someone coax a plant to grow still looked like a genuine miracle. Sensing water, or purifying it, or manipulating it felt as common as clay, by comparison.

She couldn't feel Mireille's Talent any more than the farmers could; to them, it was just a fancy light show and a budding baby plant, growing as fast as a bird taking wing. She had to use her five physical senses to assess when the work was nearly over. The plant's growth slowed, its spade-shaped leaves bright and downy, spotted with bunches of small white flowers. When Mireille pulled her hands out of the pot, she clutched two golden potatoes, each so large she could barely get her fingers around it.

"There's more in there," she said, her voice reedy with fatigue. "Six or eight. I need a break, I think."

She pushed herself away from the pot and let the crouch decay into a sit. She noticed Rhia and gave her a weak smile.

The two farmers moved in to carefully lift the pot. Rhia guessed from their strain that it was heavier than it had been when they started. The plant bowed as the farmers moved it into a line with a dozen other pots, each one boasting its own plant. The farthest ones on the end were beginning to wrinkle and sag, leaves going yellow. White petals littered the floor around the pots. They were dying as fast as they had been forced to grow.

"Good morning, Courier," Mireille said. "Did you sleep well?"

"Did you do all this yourself?" Rhia jerked her chin at the line of plants.

"I did." Mireille levered herself off the ground with a grunt, dusting her hands on her robe.

"I need to talk to you about something."

"Sure. Come out with me; I need a breath of air."

Mireille was moving slowly, taking small steps. When she reached the wall, she put a hand on it for balance. Rhia recognized the wash of fatigue that came after a strong exercise of Talent and experienced a twinge of sympathy and distress.

Rhia shouldered the door open and held it for the other woman. As she shut it behind them, she saw one of the farmers thrust his hands into the pot, digging methodically. Soil bled up around his wrists as he seized the plant's central stem and tugged it out of the pot. The raw roots shivered, fine as hair, as he shook dirt clods away from the potatoes.

It was just a plant, but there was something brutal in how he handled it. Rhia was unsettled for reasons she couldn't say, then thought tempering and turned away.

"It's not enough to feed everyone," Mireille said. "But I'm trying."

"It's heavy work regardless," Rhia said, distracted. "Look, last night something happened—"

"Mireille!"

A skinny teenage girl pounded down a track between two fields, waving. Her oversized sandals slapped the earth in rhythm with the gold-brown curls bouncing around her stricken face.

"Sorry, excuse me." Mireille visibly drew the mantle of Temple about herself as the girl approached—calm, authoritative, safe. The girl shuddered to a halt before them, barely spared a nod for the stranger from out of town, and tried to stammer out her news between gulps for air.

"My idiot brother—he got some guys along with him—gonna go look for Tansin—down the road. Think they'll be gone for days. Won't hear no about it. Idiot. I thought maybe—you could talk to him? They're going now."

Two lines notched deeply into the corners of Mireille's mouth. "I see. Thanks for telling me, Sofie. I'll come straightaway."

She set off without a word to Rhia, who trotted after her.

"What's the problem?" Rhia asked as they fell into step

together. There was a particular pace of a Priest moving to resolve a problem—smooth and fast but unruffled, not urgent. Alongside Mireille, Rhia rediscovered it. They glided down the path in the bright sun like two girl-friends taking a brisk stroll.

"Sofie's brother Rensoa fancied himself in love with Tansin, before she disappeared."

"I met Rensoa yesterday. He seemed . . . willful."

"That's a word for it." Mireille's face was set in disapproval. "He's been causing all kinds of grief to his family, insisting they drop everything and look for her. He's out every day with the search parties when truly, he's needed at home. His and Sofie's parents are aging, and they're trying to get the crops into pots so I can bloom them before they die in the dry ground. Rensoa and Sofie are young and strong. Every pair of hands makes a difference."

Rhia blew her bangs off her forehead. Maybe it wasn't the right time to mention her ransacked house. The sun was only getting higher. "Should I leave you to it?"

"No, actually, please come. You were out there yesterday, you might be able to help convince them."

She had no idea what she could possibly say to convince a group of teenage boys, but she found herself going along anyway.

A small group of young men had gathered on the edge of town near the farm fields, sitting under a tree in various states of preparation for a journey. Two were shoving hand tools into leather knapsacks; a third rolled a loaf of bread in a napkin. The fourth was Rensoa, and he was arguing with Sofie.

"What's going on here?" Mireille's calm, clear voice cut through the noise like a stone thrown into a still pond.

Rensoa broke away from his sister. "We're going to look for Tansin." His face screwed up with defiance.

"Your families need you," Mireille said.

"She needs us," Rensoa said. "She's out there, and we'll find her."

"She's not. We searched everywhere. You wouldn't get any farther than we already have in a day."

Rensoa waved a hand at the others and their preparations. "That's why we're taking supplies, so we can be out longer."

Mireille gave an almost imperceptible sigh. If Rhia hadn't been standing right next to her, she wouldn't have noticed it. From this distance, she could see the net of fine lines creeping out from the corners of the acolyte's eyes. Nearly hidden in the sleeves of her robe, her fingers trembled. She was exhausted.

"You won't get far with that," Rhia said quietly. As the stranger here, all she had to do was speak and she had their attention. "Those tools won't help you on the road. And only one loaf?" She shook her head. "You need more food, good shoes, and lots of water."

The young man with the loaf of bread looked at his bundle and frowned. "We'll . . . we'll find water on the prairie."

"You won't," Rhia said. "I'm a Water Talent, raised in the faith and Temple-trained. If there was water in the ground, I'd know it."

That was a slight exaggeration; she could only sense water within a quarter mile or so, but she figured a bit of exaggeration was due if it kept these kids at home.

"Bullshit," one of the kids muttered, loud enough to prompt a scandalized squawk from Mireille.

"On my honor," Rhia said. She directed her next statement at Rensoa: "How do you think I found that spring yesterday, when we were out searching? I could feel it coming out of the earth."

Mireille must have been surprised to hear all this, but her Priest face didn't slip and her voice stayed level. "You heard her. Courier Silver has been on the road; she knows what she's talking about."

The title *Courier* sent a flutter of recognition through the group. The word carried its own legend, one of endless roaming, self-reliance, lonely voyages far from home. Rhia felt their awe and took advantage of it.

"It's bone-dry in every direction," she said. "There are beasts and snakes. No shelter. No food. You have to sleep cold, because lighting a fire could burn out half the prairie. Your friend wouldn't want you risking your skins out looking for her."

"She could be out there hurt!"

If she went out and got hurt two weeks ago, her bones are scattered all over the grass by now. Rhia didn't speak the words, but from the looks on the other boys' faces, it was clear they were all thinking the same thing she was. Everyone but Rensoa.

"She didn't get hurt," Sofie said quietly. "The greyhowler got her, and if you go it'll get you too."

"Shut up, Sofie!" Rensoa clearly knew he was losing ground, and he whirled on his sister with more anger than was justified. "The greyhowler's made up!"

"It's *not*," Sofie insisted. "You *know* it's not, we heard it—"

"She could just have run away," Rhia cut in. "She wanted to be a Priest, right? Maybe she left for a Temple. For all we know, I passed her on the road days ago, going out of town as I was coming in."

That prompted a murmur of discussion from Rensoa's friends.

"If you wait a few more days," Mireille said "Micah will be back. He'll know what to do. He'll put together more search parties; we'll do it properly."

"How can you say we should wait, when we could go now? I thought you *liked* Tansin. She was your *friend*."

"It's not safe out on the prairie, Ren."

"You don't believe this bullshit about the greyhowler," Rensoa snapped. "You're a Priest!"

"I believe the things that I see, and what I see now is how badly your family needs your help."

"*Tansin* needs my—"

"Ren," one of his friends said timidly. "Maybe we could wait another day."

"Forget all of you, then!" Rensoa shouted. His face was ruddy and thunderous. "Tansin is out there alone and I'm the only one that cares at all!"

He threw down his backpack and ran back toward the town.

Sofie watched him, worry writ large on her face. "He'll be back out here tomorrow." she said to Mireille.

"Then we'll have this conversation again tomorrow," Mireille said firmly. "We can't have people running off right now, especially with someone already missing."

Rensoa's friends gathered up his dropped belongings and the teenagers slowly headed back into town. Sofie squeezed Mireille's hands in thanks and trotted after them.

Rhia looked at Mireille, impressed. She didn't think she'd have been able to straddle the line between firm and compassionate like that, especially not with a group of teenagers. She swiped discreetly at the sweat rolling into her waistband. "Do you do this a lot? Go into Priest mode and talk people out of doing stupid shit?"

"More now than two weeks ago. Everyone's temperature is running a little hot since the headman left." Mireille tipped her gaze toward Rhia, and it was cold and practical and full of unspoken things. "Are you really Water Talented?"

Rhia set her jaw. "I'm sorry I didn't mention it earlier, given the drought and all. I didn't think there was anything I could do to help, and I—I tend to keep it private."

"Were you really raised in the Temple?"

"I was."

"What degree's your Talent?"

"Seventh."

Mireille's eyes widened. "Gods above, why aren't you a Priest?"

Because they didn't want me. Rhia felt her upper lip pull off her teeth, shoved it back down. "Lots of reasons."

"Please." Mireille caught Rhia's wrist. "I beg you. All I can do is grow plants. Please. You can search for water for us. There may be something in the ground, something none of us would know about. You could find it." *You could save us,* was implied so clearly she might as well have said it aloud.

Rhia shook her head. "There's not. I felt for it the night I got here, and again last night at the spring. There's nothing. The ground's as dry as soot."

"But that was clear on the other side of town! Maybe out here—you could just *try . . .* "

Rhia could see hope warring with reason on Mireille's face and grimaced. She didn't want to be the one to break the acolyte's heart, but maybe it would be better to resolve the question quickly so they could concentrate on coping with reality.

"Of course." Rhia took a seat under the scrubby tree. If she'd thought this would take more than a minute, she would have suggested going back to town, but the ground was so sere her mouth got dry thinking about it. This was going to be fruitless.

She closed her eyes, called up her Talent, and—

There was water in the earth nearby.

Somewhere to the south, there was a deep bulb of water, ripe and fresh as a melon. Rhia's senses drank it like she was one of the town's parched plants.

It only took a heartbeat to return to the dry ground under the tree. She blinked up at Mireille as her Talent withdrew into her body. She could see the pulse of liquid in Mireille's body emitting marbled light until she rubbed her eyes.

"Mireille." She pointed. "I was wrong. There's something that way."

Mireille's face lifted, then fell as she followed along Rhia's pointed finger. "You're pointing toward the well-house. There's water cached in barrels there, but the well itself is dry."

"Yeah, well, it might be dry on the surface, but there's water underneath it."

"Really?"

"Yes." Rhia ran her dry tongue over her teeth and levered herself to her feet . Her head swam. It was dastardly hot. "Do you have anything to dri—"

"Back in town." Mireille's face was knit up in concern. "We should get you somewhere cool."

"I'll be fine in a minute." Rhia put her back against the tree and drank air deep into her belly. The prairie blazed blonde under the sun. A column of dust lifted off the horizon. "I just got a little swimmy. You know how it goes."

"I know?" Mireille laughed sharply. "I'm a fourth degree. I barely qualify for Priesthood."

Better for you if you didn't. "We should go to the well-house. Might be I can do something for it."

"Are you sure?" Mireille touched Rhia's arm gently. "I don't want you passing out. Let's go back to town first, let you get your feet back under you."

"Thanks. I'm fine. I got too hot for a minute."

"I really think—"

The column of dust was thickening. Shapes were visible in it— a person walking alongside a bigger blob. A cart? Rhia squinted. "Look."

The column resolved—one person walking, one driving a small cart pulled by a donkey. Mireille's name ghosted across the open space between them, distorted by the breeze. The walker waved.

The acolyte turned and her face lit up. Ten years of age dropped off her face.

"Micah," she breathed.

The headman had returned.

"There's no drought in Columb. They can pump it out on the damn ground just to see the splash."

Headman Micah Arboles sat in the front room of his house, where a makeshift office shared the space with a humble kitchen. It was one of the few two-room houses in town. Rhia presumed the closed door behind the desk led to a bedroom. Rhia, Mireille, and the headman's husband, Priano, were positioned in spots around the small room.

The letter Rhia had brought from Tellemont sat in the center of Micah's desk—sweat-smudged, wax seal blurred from being pressed against her body for two days. The gold- and silver-banded purple ribbon fastened around it was dingy and wrinkled. On reflex, she felt a kind of professional embarrassment.

"It's not just their wells are full," Micah continued. "I woke in the morning to dew on the wagon. The season is turning. There's water out there."

Rhia sipped from a cup, tasted the piney pitch tang the water had picked up inside the cask. It made her think of tall dark trees in winter. Mireille had pulled the water fresh from one of the casks the headman had returned with and pressed it into Rhia's hand, her expression silencing Rhia's protests before she could utter them.

The headman and his husband had gone into the village and returned with a third man, large and bald, who was currently unloading casks of water from the back of the wagon into a storehouse. It would be enough for the town to drink for another week or so, and then they would have to return for more. There was nothing with which to water the plants.

"Is that normal?" Mireille asked. "For there to be a drought that's only local to one small area?"

"It's damned unusual, is what it is. I got hopeful when I saw it, came back thinking it might've cleared up here." Micah ran a damp cloth over the back of his neck and dropped it on the desk. Dust was set into the lines in his forehead like a cat's stripes.

"It's no better," Mireille said. "And still no sign of Tansin. People are . . . getting unsettled."

Micah sighed. "Can't blame them. Still hearing the greyhowler, I take it."

"Every night."

Micah let out a sigh and leveled his eyes on Rhia. "And what's your story? Mireille says you've a Water Talent. Did the Temple send you?"

"I'm a Courier. I do have a Water Talent, yes, but I didn't know about your trouble until I got here. I just came with a letter, same as anyone would."

"I see." He steepled his fingers in front of his face, then dropped his head against them as if the muscles of his neck had gotten too tired to hold it up. "I suppose that was too much to hope for, anyway, that the Temple would send someone when we already have Mireille here. It's just that Tansin was Water Talented too. Only person in the town with any lick of Talent to speak of, albeit not much."

"I know," Rhia said. "I met your vow-father yesterday, Tansin's uncle Creff. He told me a lot about her. Wanted to be a Priest, right?"

Mireille made a soft noise of distress. Rhia cast a wordless question across the room to her, but she looked away.

"You can understand how it might seem especially dire, the loss of a Water Talent at a time like this. If there's anything you can do for us now, we'd all be very much obliged."

Rhia looked again at the letter on the desk, then, fleetingly, out the window to the horizon.

Her job was done. She badly wanted to leave, to be free of this place and away . . . but Tansin was still missing and there was a monster in the streets at night and the town was dying of thirst. It was possible she could do something about one of those things, at least.

Away would always be there.

"Of course." She settled her weight back on her heels. "I'd be happy to take a look at your wellhouse. I sensed water in the ground, earlier, and Mireille said it might be around there."

"That would be terrific." He levered himself out of the chair with a muffled groan.

"Do you want to—" Rhia jerked her chin at the letter on the table.

"We should go straightaway," Mireille interrupted. "If no one minds. Seems water's the most important thing—I think if we could return from the wellhouse with something to show, it would raise the spirits in town quite a lot."

"It couldn't hurt," Micah's husband agreed. "Folks are smeared thin."

"That they are." Pulling open a drawer in the desk, Micah slid the letter into it and turned the key in the latch. "Plenty of time for correspondence after the sun's down."

Rhia tried to quash her indignation. She had carried this letter for a month—across many leagues!—and it stung to have it disregarded so easily. But they were right. The possibility of water outweighed word from out of town, whatever that word might be.

The four of them left for the wellhouse, Rhia throwing a last look over her shoulder at where the letter lay locked in the headman's desk.

Fresh footprints marked the dusty road, laid atop yesterday's swooping markings. Someone was going back and forth from here, although to what purpose, Rhia couldn't guess. *Maybe just some poor optimist checking the well every day.*

Seen up close, the wellhouse was identical in shape and construction to the potting sheds where Mireille had grown potato plants that morning, but much bigger. A narrow length of pipe stuck a handspan out of the ground next to the wall, drawing her attention because she couldn't readily identify its purpose. She knew a lot about water, but not much about wells.

A vent? Something to let out air from underground, keep the well flowing smoothly?

Rhia followed the headman and acolyte into the dark, musty space. The room sloped down to a round, drain-like opening rimmed by a knee-high wall of stone. The floor was packed earth.

The well itself was a pupil, velvety black.

The hair on the back of Rhia's neck stood up and she fought the urge to put her back against the wall. Her Talent tingled. She felt an apprehension too dim and bleak for words. There was a gulping tension in the space like a hand around her throat. She could smell cobwebs and dirt, but no water. The air was too hot, too still. Her imagination tore loose and fed her the metallic flavor of a mouthful of dirt, gave her the claustrophobic all-over pressure along her limbs and torso that would come from being buried alive, clutched in the heart of the earth.

She glanced over at Mireille. The acolyte was grim-faced, looking at the open well as if its mouth would belch up answers. Rhia wondered if Mireille felt the same sense of gut-deep unease she did.

"How's it work?" Micah asked, and Mireille jumped. Rhia realized her hands had locked into fists and forced her knuckles to unwind.

"Do you have to say a prayer or . . ." He seemed unaffected by the tension in the room.

Rhia cleared her throat, wished belatedly that she'd thought to bring her waterskin. "I just need some quiet," she said.

The soil around the well was cool and dusty. She felt a chill through the thin linen of her trousers when she sat cross-legged on the floor. Weird that it would be so cold, when the air in the wellhouse was so stuffy, but she accepted it as an unanticipated blessing and closed her eyes.

The bell of water rang deep and low beneath her seat. She had been right, sitting out under the dying tree. There was water here, and in abundance. She dropped her awareness out of her body and plunged toward the water like a stone, sinking fast and deep. It was an aquifer accumulated in decades or even centuries of precipitation. It felt as old as the continent. She sent her awareness through it, mineral-rich and ice-cold—a primordial cache of life. It spread out below the water table in all directions around the wellhouse. It could hold a family of whales. It should have lasted for years.

Rhia opened her eyes. "There's plenty of water down there."

"Then what's the problem?" Micah asked. "Do we need to dig deeper?"

She shook her hair off her forehead and flattened her lips. "Let me see."

The water blossomed against the bottom of the well basin, lingering just beneath the surface of the earth. There was a smaller cache of water nearby—a few feet under some of the storage barrels. Rhia ignored it, chalking it up to an errant patch of groundwater, something that trickle-fed the aquifer. Ultimately, there was no reason for the well to have run dry. The aquifer was full. In her mind, she could picture the bottom of the well puncturing the top of the hidden reservoir.

Calling water was one of the first things you learned in the Temple. The natural affinity between your Talent and the element formed a kind of leash, and all you had to do was tug gently—

She beckoned. Then cajoled. Then *pulled*.

The water didn't come.

She rocked back on her hips, puffing out air. She was sweating.

"The water's down there, but it won't come. It's like it's blocked or something. Was there an earthquake recently?"

The words felt stupid coming out of her mouth. Of course there wouldn't have been an earthquake out here, on the glass-flat prairie. Micah and Mireille were both shaking their heads. Mireille's face was drawn and pale. Rhia felt the acolyte's eyes on her like physical weight. *She must think I'm this place's last chance.*

Fine. She fisted her hands in the fabric of her trousers and went deep. She dropped her Talent down into the depths of the aquifer, distributing her awareness as much as she could—holding as much water as her mind would carry. She *pushed*, shoving a bulb of water against the bottom of the well, imagining it breaching the dry earth. Bubbling up.

The bulb squished against a flat surface as immovable and impermeable as obsidian.

She pushed again.

No water came.

Rhia shrunk her focus to an armspan or so and, exhaling a slow breath, took the ever-moving water in her Talent's grip and slowed it down. Water was perpetually in motion. Even laying still in a glass, there were tiny droplets, smaller than the eye could see, circulating together. When the droplets slowed, they locked together. Chilled. Froze.

Rhia formed a fist-sized block of ice in the aquifer and pounded it against the bottom of the well. Twice. Harder. *Again.* The solid block remained, unmoving.

Rhia's upper lip curled. She was a seventh-degree Talent and had been in line for the Priesthood. She could pull the rain from thunderclouds. She had halted a flash flood. At no time in her life had any water disobeyed her.

She shoved her will into the ice and *pushed*.

There was a splash and gurgle. Water splattered the top of her head. When she opened her eyes, the wellhouse ceiling was wet and dripping. She had pulled the water up with such force it formed a brief geyser.

Mireille was on the wall around the well, braced on her hands and peering into the depths. Micah seized a wooden bucket on a line and tossed it into the opening. It splashed.

He spun, a look of elation on his face. "It's filling!"

Rhia was dizzy from her exertion, but she managed a nod and smile.

Mireille turned away from the well. Relief and worry chased each other across her features. "Is it . . . fixed? Will the water come back now?"

Rhia stretched carefully and prepared to stand, mindful of stiff joints. She felt poorly aligned with her body, like her consciousness was off-set from her limbs by a handspan in every direction. "There's plenty of water down there, like I said. Something was just blocking it."

A complex mixture of expressions danced over the acolyte's features, but Rhia had no time to inquire. Micah charged between them and took her hands, pulling her to her feet with the restrained exuberance a large dog develops after it breaks one too many ceramics in the house.

"Courier Silver, we owe you a debt we can't begin to repay." His restraint ran out and he crushed Rhia in a hug. "You'll eat the finest dinner we can provide tonight, sleep in the best bed—"

"Please," she wheezed, and he released her. Rhia took a step back, brushing dust from her clothes, and put her hands between them in a gesture that discouraged further mauling. "*Please.* Don't go out of your way, I only did what it's decent to do—"

"*Let those among you who the gods' gifts elevate reach back and lift all folk beside them in turn,*" Mireille murmured in reflex.

"*. . . that all may in joyful service bring the gods' kingdom to life on earth,*" Rhia rattled off the rest of the verse. "Yeah. Exactly. It's just what you do." Also, she hated being made a fuss over.

"You must stay at least another night, then." Micah was frenzied with joy. "The town will want to celebrate. We have some casks of cider we've been holding back. Join us for that, at least."

A smile quirked onto Rhia's mouth without her say-so. His relief was infectious. Draining tension unlocked her shoulders. "All right, okay. But no longer. I have other deliveries waiting for me by now, I'm sure."

"Of course, of course." Micah looped an arm around Mireille's shoulders and gestured them all out of the wellhouse. "You know, if the well keeps running I bet people start coming back to town. Now all we need is for Tansin to come wandering out of the prairie and things might even start getting back to normal."

As the wellhouse door shut behind them, Rhia heard the water glugging into the bottom of the well with a sound like sobs.

෪

Just outside, they found a man stooped beside the well-house wall. He had dirty fingers and a trowel in one hand. He was carefully scooping and chipping away at the dry earth, excavating something.

"Are you clearing the pipe, Will?" Micah asked, then turned to Rhia and Mireille and explained: "There's some pipeworks here that run between the wellhouse and the spring."

The man stood, pulling his shirt straight. As the collar moved, Rhia caught a glimpse of a jagged white scar just below his clavicle. He was big, broad-shouldered, and bald, with deep smile lines notched on either side of his mouth. Belatedly, she recognized him from her first night in Cerretour as a member of the search party she had seen by the dry spring.

The man smiled bashfully. "I thought if you were able to restore the water, someone should make sure the pipe's clear."

Rhia squinted in the direction of the dry spring, but she couldn't see it from here. The gold prairie and dark-brown town shimmied in the heat waves like a dog's back with fleas. "You want to fill the spring from the well?"

"That was my thought," he said. "It would give people a couple places to draw from, maybe a second reservoir in case the well runs dry again. Did you restore the water?"

"She did. She's a seventh-degree Talent," Mireille said, with a hint of pride.

The man opened his mouth and Rhia interrupted to forestall what she feared was an overflow of Temple-inflected praise. "How did you know I was going to—?"

"A gaggle of children wandered past my house, chattering about how Cerretour's new visitor is a Courier, and a Temple-trained Water Talent to boot. I'm sure half the town knows by now."

Rhia sighed with such exasperation that both men grinned.

"News travels fast in a town this size," Micah said.

Rhia gestured at the half-buried length of ceramic set into the ground. "How full does the well have to be for the water to hit the pipe?"

"Quite full, I imagine. The pipe is barely under the topsoil." He tapped his foot against the pipe. "I'm no pipe-fitter, but my da was, and near as I can tell it looks sound. I don't even know if it will work, if I'm honest . . . but I hope it will. Mostly I just like having something to do."

"Will's a helper," Mireille said, in the tone of someone whose daily work involved dealing with a lot of well-intentioned hindrances.

"That I am," the man said, smiling broadly.

"So what's the plan here?" Micah asked. "You know the pipe is intact . . ."

"Aye, so . . . I guess I head over to the spring and wait."

Rhia's reserves of Talent were rebounding from her exercise with the ice block in the aquifer. She probed her inner well, testing it the way she would a warmed-up muscle, and found it deep enough.

"Let me help you." She gestured at the vent pipe sticking out of the ground on the other side of the path. "There's clearly some kind of system built here already. It might be to regulate pressure on the pipes. I can bring up some water and see if we can get it flowing on its own. It'll be faster than waiting for the well to fill high enough to do it naturally."

"Would you? I'd be very much obliged."

"Rhia . . ." Mireille's eyes flickered to the vent pipe and back to the other woman. Concern knitted her brows together. "You did tremendous work in the wellhouse. You must be tired. I don't think . . ."

"I'm fine. You were up before dawn growing potatoes," Rhia pointed out. "You're likely more tired than I am."

Politeness kept her from pointing out that her Talent was much stronger than Mireille's, so instead they had silent argument by eye contact. Mireille broke off first, took a long look at the wellhouse, and, with a shake of her head, visibly came to a conclusion.

"Are you sure you can make it back to town on your own?"

"It's like a quarter-mile." Rhia flapped her hand at Mireille. "Get."

"Come on," Micah said, and put a guiding hand on the acolyte's shoulder. "You're too young to be everyone's mother."

Mireille was clearly still worried, but she gave the bald man a polite smile and left with Micah.

The bald man watched them head down the path and ran the back of his hand over his sweat-dampened brow. "I appreciate your offer, Courier. It's only getting hotter out here. Will this really work?"

"It should if the spring is lower than where the pipe starts here," Rhia said. "The pipe may need a vent where air can get in, too. Managing water flow without Talent can be tricky. There's something called the siphon effect, we learned about in . . . Well, I'm trying to say we won't know unless we try."

"Then let's try." He wiped a dirty palm on his trousers and offered her his hand. "I'm Will. Will Cordance."

She took it. "Rhia Silver."

"Would you like to go back inside?" He asked. "It'll be easier if you're closer to the water."

It was weird that he knew that, but Rhia shrugged it off. She looked at the closed wellhouse door with some trepidation. "I suppose," she said.

It felt worse to be alone in the room than it had in the company of others. The glugging sound of water filling the well had slowed, gaining depth and richness like a rising bread dough.

Rhia dropped the bucket in and listened. The time between release and splash was shorter. *The well's filling quickly.* She frowned. *You probably didn't even have to come in here. The water would have hit the pipe on its own soon enough.*

After an interval, she hauled on the rope with more force than she needed, venting tension through her triceps and shoulders. She was mad at herself for being scared.

She set the dripping bucket on the well's stone wall, plunged her cupped hands in, and drank. The water was cool and tinny with minerals. Eager to be done, she used the fresh draught of cool liquid running through her body to connect to its source below the earth and pulled a lean tentacle of water up from the well basin. It didn't take long to find the opening where the pipe let out into the well. She used her Talent to thread maybe a gallon of water into the pipe and when she felt it begin to move on its own, flowing along a barely-perceptible slope away from the wellhouse, she released her grip on it.

That's that. She came back into her body, dumped the remainder of the water in the bucket back into the well, and headed for the door.

A whisper of sound stopped her. She tilted her head, hound-like, and listened. Neither the dark wood walls nor the shaggy earthen floor gave up any secrets.

It was so faint. She could have imagined it.

The sound came again. It was a word, or a phrase. It was nearly a voice. It was impossible to say if she was really hearing it, or if her mind was playing tricks on her.

It's like someone's crying for help.

The room yawned around her. Her nightmares loomed large.

Maybe it's me. Maybe I'm the one crying for help.

She was tiny and afraid, locked in a predator's jaws. The greyhowler. The well was a gullet. Primordial digestive sounds came from beneath the earth.

All the hair on her arms was standing up. She broke for the door.

Will looked up as she emerged from the dark room, blinking owlishly in the sun. "Did you do it?"

She checked over her shoulder once, and shut the door firmly on all of it: the filling well and the whispering sound and her fear.

"Yeah," she said. "I did it. Let's go."

They set out into the prairie together, grass whisking around their thighs. Rhia's Talent followed the track of pipe as the water flowed toward the dry spring. She kept a mental eye on it as they forged through the uncut grassland. It was another clear-sky day, and her nose sang with the sweet tang of drying grass. Insects buzzed. Birds sang in their hidden nests, falling silent as the two walkers approached.

Will must have been able to tell that something was bothering her. He let a few minutes of silence pass, then offered a gentle overture at conversation: "I have to say, I've never met a Courier before. One trained in the Temple, no less."

"I'm probably the only one." Rhia said grimly, her mind still half on the sound she might have heard. *I was alone in there. It wasn't a voice . . . but then what was it?*

"How do you get into this line of work?"

"By leaving the Temple and needing to eat," she said, more short with him than she meant to be. Chagrined, she softened her tone and continued: "I started as a Runner in a city when I was a teenager, same as anyone would, and worked my way up."

"I can appreciate the desire to travel," Will said. "I do a fair amount of it myself... It can make for a lonely life at times."

"You're not from Cerretour?"

"Not originally, no. I've been here for a few weeks, but I'm from all over."

Rhia snorted. "Then what are you still doing here? If I hadn't needed to give a letter specifically to Micah, I would have cleared out at first light the morning after I got here. No water, missing person, someone tearing up the inside of my house..."

"Someone broke into your house?"

"Yeah, last night. Went through all my stuff and didn't take anything."

"Why on earth would they do that?"

She shrugged. "They must've thought I was carrying something valuable. It happens to Couriers sometimes. But all I had was a letter for Micah, and they didn't get it."

"Hrm." A fierce expression stole over his face like a thundercloud and he looked at the ground, thinking deeply.

"Hey, don't worry about it," Rhia said, confused by the intensity of his reaction. "And anyway, it doesn't matter—I'm leaving first thing in the morning. But why are you still here? Oh, do you feel like you can't leave? I guess you wouldn't feel safe, setting out alone with the . . ." She gestured broadly at the prairie, a little embarrassed to be referring, even obliquely, to a monster she claimed not to believe in.

"What, the greyhowler?" That pulled him out of the brown study and he shook his head with a chuckle. "Gods, no. That's not real."

"What?" Rhia stopped dead and stared at him. "I mean, yeah, of course it's not real. But everyone seems to believe in it."

"Well, why don't you?"

"Because . . . I mean, every place has something, a tall-bear or a skin thief or a look-away man." She was flustered, hearing echoes of her fruitless discussion with Creff the previous day. "In the Temple when I was a kid, they used to tell us about how in ancient times, priests would tame this thing called the lusus mendace and it would hunt down dishonesty."

He shrugged.

"You really don't believe," she said, and laughed a little, surprised by how relieved she felt. "Thank gods for that. Everyone in Cerretour seems to believe in this monster, except maybe Mireille, and there are these noises at night . . . I was starting to . . . I think I needed—"

"Reassurance?"

"Maybe." She smiled sheepishly. "Maybe just to stay grounded in what's real."

They started walking again. Rhia kicked over a rock, thinking.

"I think that's part of what makes stories like this creepy. The ones about monsters and boogeymen and such. And it keeps them creepy even after you're an adult," she said, working the conclusion out as it occurred to her. "They have enough in common that they always sound familiar, even the first time you hear them."

"As if there's a truth to them that exists whether you believe or not," Will observed.

"Yeah, exactly." Rhia shook her head. "Stupid."

"Now Courier, that's a bit unfair, isn't it?" He asked. "It's human nature to see the patterns between things. And it's certainly not stupid to know what scares you. It's human nature to remember our fears, too. Sharing stories like the greyhowler, the lusus mendace, isn't so different from warning others about packs of wolves or bandits or landslides. Whether the monster is real or not, talking about it is part of how we keep each other alive."

Rhia settled her eyes on the dun-colored scrape at the edge of the prairie. The dry spring had come into view. "I prefer to think for myself."

They kept walking. Sweat ran down her spine. The sun laid another layer of burn across her reddened shoulders.

The thread of water thinned out as they got closer to the spring. Either the downward slope wasn't steep enough or the pipes were leaking.

Will had just asked her a question. "Sorry. What?"

"I was wondering if you ever missed the community of being in the Temple, as opposed to being out here in the world, on your own."

"I don't really think about it," she lied.

"Of course not," he said, so quickly she knew she hadn't hidden her discomfort with the topic well enough. "There are so many ways to have a fulfilling life."

Rhia remembered carrying a bucket of grain through the chilly morning farmyard to feed the sheep. Mud and shit squishing between her toes, the bucket banging against her shins. The complaining sheep forming an absurd chorus for the Priests, who were warm and dry inside, droning on in an interminable monotonous prayer.

"Life in the Temple isn't always as fulfilling as you might think."

Will laughed, startling her and scaring a half-dozen birds out of a nearby stand of scrub brush. They flew together like they had one body, white bellies flashing in unison, swooping in a tight arc between the bushes and the sky. They vanished into the grasses and the air filled with peeping and chattering warning calls.

Rhia and Will watched, struck silent.

"And cooped up in the Temple," he said softly as the birdsong faded "you don't get to see little miracles like that."

He spoke so softly, he could have been speaking to himself. An expression of genuine wonder was on his face. Rhia smiled. All of a sudden, she liked him.

She had lost the thread of water, she realized, but they weren't far from the spring now.

The grass parted and broke and they stood beside the dry spring. In broad daylight, Rhia could see where a time-worn length of red ceramic pipe jutted out of the earth and into the basin.

It was dry as a dead man's teeth. Not a drop fell onto the dusty springbed.

"Drat," Will said. "Well. It was worth a try, I suppose."

Rhia stared into the hollow basin. She'd known it was unlikely that the water would make it this far down the pipe, but she was more disappointed than she'd expected. "I suppose."

The bald man seemed unaffected by their failed experiment. "Cheer up, Courier. The well is filling, at any rate. Let's head back to town."

That night, there was a celebration. After the sun went down, the people of Cerretour hung little gas lanterns across the main street, spaced at regular intervals so the air was lit by a soft yellow glow. In front of the headman's house they lay a table with crops Mireille had force-grown, six crispy-skinned chickens, and dusty bottles of plum wine. The headman himself rolled a cask of cider out of the storehouse, and the one bar in town unbolted its doors, spreading its meager collection of benches and stools in the middle of the street for people to congregate around.

There was a sense of the town taking its first breath in weeks.

Rhia watched the festivities unfold, her butt parked against the porch railing outside a nearby house. She had a plate piled with chicken and fruit in one hand and a frankly enormous glass of cider tucked in the crook of her arm. She drank from the headman's own guesting-cup, carved and enameled, the one concession she'd made to his desire to celebrate her.

Rhia kept Micah from telling the town about her part in restoring the water supply. The populace accepted her as she was, an observer of an unlooked-for miracle: the return of the headman and the return of their water on the selfsame day.

Folks had been running in and out of the wellhouse all day, filling buckets and cookpots and pitchers and waterskins from the replenished well. It had taken a few hours for the line to clear enough for Rhia to claim her own tub of water and carry it back to her little borrowed house. When she got there she had pulled the shutters closed, stripped bare, and washed and splashed with giddy abandon. Every surface in the house was damp. She kept touching her hair to feel its softness. She was clean, really clean, for the first time in weeks, and that felt as good as a fine meal and a cider from the headman's guesting-cup.

A man produced a fiddle and struck up a cheery, slightly wild tune. A woman joined in on a round drum with rattles set into its frame. While no one seemed drunk or exuberant enough to dance yet, the night was clearly going in that direction. Toes tapping, Rhia pinched an ambitious portion of chicken into her mouth with her fingers, checked to make sure no one was looking, and wiped greasy fingers on her pantleg. She was suddenly ravenous. Counting back the days, she realized she hadn't eaten a hot meal in a week.

She kicked her feet up onto a rock and settled on the porch rail. One couple, then another, then a group of five, whirled out into the flat-packed road in front of the musicians. A roil of dust lifted up to their knees as they danced. Someone was laughing. The music was good. Rhia was getting drunk.

Something moved in the shadows between two houses. Lanternlight reflected off two bright eyes, and Rhia startled, almost dropping her plate. Not the greyhowler, though; these eyes were higher, reflected white, not yellow. Human.

Rensoa appeared from the shadows between the houses, a rumpled dark-colored sweater camouflaging his body until he got closer. The lanternlight picked out the gawky points of his elbows and cheekbones. His hands were shoved in his pockets, his back stooped like an old man's. Rhia wasn't sure if he'd noticed her or not. His face was screwed tight with resentment. She remembered his outrage that morning—his obvious sense of pain, of being unheard.

Rensoa spat discreetly in the direction of the celebration and spun on his heel to depart. Facing Rhia, he saw her watching him, and directed an especially sharp glare in her direction.

"Tansin's prob'ly *dead*," he muttered as he slumped by. "Could be buried under your feet. You don't even care."

Rhia figured any protestation would be a waste of breath.

"Can't even talk Mireille into looking. Not this morning, not tonight. If the greyhowler got Tansin, it won't stop."

"Thought you didn't believe in the greyhowler," Rhia offered quietly. She could feel the deep vein of hurt he was bleeding from, and wanted to staunch it.

"Doesn't matter what I believe, does it? Nothing I say is gonna make folks care about finding her."

Rhia blew her bangs off her forehead. "Trust me, kid, this isn't what not caring looks like."

He sneered and stumped into the darkness. "Careful on the road as you leave, Courier."

Teenagers. Celandine had said that *teen* was an old-fashioned word that meant *grief*. When Rhia had been his age, she'd been fleeing the Temple, certain there was no one to trust, no one who would fully understand her again. Old enough to make permanent decisions, young enough not to understand that's what they were.

An idea stirred in the cauldron of her mind, a concoction of recent information and subconscious analysis rising and blending together. She thought of Tansin, old enough to want to be a Priest, young enough she wouldn't hear no about it. She thought of herself, running away. There was a connection there, but she couldn't get a hold of it. She slugged back a gulp of cider.

"Good evening, Courier."

Will Cordance materialized out of the darkness. A fresh shave and scrubbed face had given him the appearance of a large, friendly baby. He carried a wooden mug that was tiny in his hands.

"Hullo Will," she said, mouth full of chicken.

"Mind if I join you?"

"Be my guest," she said. The railing muttered a complaint as it accepted his bulk.

"You look quite content with yourself," he said, smiling at her full plate and cup.

"This is the best meal I've had in weeks." It didn't feel appropriate to wipe her fingers on her trousers now that someone was sitting next to her, so she swiped them against the railing inconspicuously and went back to her food. "And have you had tried the cider? Gods damn."

"I'm content with water," he said, hoisting his mug. "An excess of drink is bad for a man."

"Good thing m'not a man, then," she said and drank more cider.

"I was wondering if you'd seen Mireille around this evening?"

"Not lately. Why?"

Will drank deep from his mug. Firelight hit and smeared in a reflection across his head. "Oh, I wanted to ask her about her work in the potting sheds. Everyone's got a story to tell, and Mireille is responsible for all the vegetables we're eating tonight. It always amazes me, what Talented people can do. *The gifts of the god-touched bloom as wildflowers, their glories manifold across the surface of the land.*"

Rhia gave him a sidelong glance. "Don't often hear scripture at a party, Will Cordance."

He smiled. "What can I say, I'm a believer. Is she doing services?"

"Yeah, dawn some days, sundown others."

"Perhaps I'll see you there, then." He levered his body off the rail and tipped his mug to her. "Nice talking to you, Courier."

Rhia nodded as he lumbered off into the evening.

See me at services? Not likely.

The night wore on. The lights got brighter and blurred, waxing into hazy spheres like tiny moons. Rhia drifted closer to the music, sat herself down on a barrel and watched the dancers, their sleeves and skirts and vests whirling. She tapped her heels against the wood happily, confident that she was far away enough from the dancing not to get pulled in by an overeager stranger.

"It's nice, isn't it?"

Mireille was suddenly beside her, a cup in her hand, twin apples glowing in her cheeks. Rhia scooted over on the barrel and patted the empty space beside her.

"Itsh nishe," Rhia agreed and realized abruptly she was drunk. "Nice. It'sss nissse."

Mireille grinned as she sat. "Careful. Cider'll get ya. They did something like this the week I got here. Big party. Next day, I wished I'd died in my sleep."

"That's what you get for getting drunk, Acolyte. *Intoshicants dull the eye to the beauty of the godsh' creation.*"

Mireille giggled delightedly. "You really *are* Temple bred, aren't you?"

"For better or worse." Rhia knocked back the last swallow of cider in the headman's guesting cup. "Someone's lookin' for you. Was earlier, anyway. Will, that big guy from the wellhouse earlier."

That seemed to land on a spot Rhia hadn't intended. Mireille's jaw set, her chin tilted. "Was he?"

"Yeah. Didn't say what for. I mean, he did. Said he wanted to hear your story or something, but what does that even mean?"

"Who knows?"

"Said he'd be at services, anyway. See you there."

"I see." She tapped her heels against the barrel, visibly pondering this until she came to a conclusion she didn't share. "I haven't seen you at services, Courier."

Rhia snorted. "That's because I don't go to services, Priest."

Mireille grinned. "Don't worry, I'm not here to shepherd your wayward soul back under the bough of the Temple. But I am curious—why did you leave?"

Rhia shook her head. A host of old memories flickered up out of the darkness and she leaned away from them like a dog at the end of a long chain.

She finally settled on: "Something bad happened. And when I said . . . nobody believed me."

"Hmm. Maybe I didn't need to ask that. Maybe I know already." Mireille drummed her heels against the wood staves of the barrel, more for the noise than in time with the music. "It's because your life in the Temple wasn't real."

"What?"

Mireille gestured with her cup out over the street, the people dancing, the dark prairie beyond. "Being out here . . . in this town, it's like suddenly everything means something. You know? Real things, the drought, people missing . . . I feel like they really need me here. I never felt like anyone needed me in the Temple. It was all . . . you know. It felt pretend, almost. Not like real life. Not helping anyone. It was hard."

Rhia's memories of life in the Temple were divided starkly into *Before* and *After*, but sheep shit aside, many of the Before memories were good: the mist rising off the pear orchards in Roundtree; the small bells ringing to summon her to prayer or chores or meditation; scrambling over the walls and rooftops of the enclosure with her foster brother; skinning her knee out in the farmyard in spring, trying to get a look at the first lambs.

She hadn't known, at the time, how sheltered she'd been. How sheltered they all were.

"I know what you mean."

"That's why I asked, when you first got here. If the Citadel had sent you. I thought you might be here to shoo me on my way."

"Hmm?" Rhia dragged herself back from memory. "To shoo you?"

"Yeah, like . . ." Mireille squirmed back and forth on the barrel. She extended her legs out and examined her toes. She suddenly looked very young. Rhia thought again of her childhood self, her skinned knees. "You know, to make me . . . Make sure I finished my roving."

Rhia snorted. "That's ridiculous. Honestly, since the first night I got here, I've wanted to leave. I don't get places like this at all. People stay in small towns like this their whole lives . . . I dunno. It makes me feel trapped, like the walls are all too close."

"Yeah, but you're a Courier. You have a professional interest in not getting trapped. It's your job to leave." She was teasing, Rhia realized, and they shared a smile. Mireille peered into the bottom of her mug, and verifying it was empty, turned her face to the lanternlight, the skirling fiddle music, the dancers. "Not me though."

When Mireille looked up into the sky, the curve of her brow was outlined by starlight.

"I love this place. They need me. All I want is to stay."

Rhia stumbled through the dark room, child-sized again, dry dirt crusting under her fingernails. Water dripped, barely audible, nowhere nearby. She couldn't find it. The air was close and dusty. Claws clicked. Something was tracing the path behind her.

The greyhowler bayed in the darkness, far out of view. The stacatto rhythm of the claws grew louder. The relative distances collided in her mind—if the greyhowler was so far away, what was approaching from behind her?

It's not the greyhowler. It's something else.

"Don't forget!" Celandine was on the other side of the room, lit from within with a ghostly white glow. "The lusus mendace hunts those who tell lies."

Rhia opened her mouth and dirt poured out.

"It's here because it smells a lie," Mireille said. Celandine had become her, or maybe Celandine had always been her. She was holding one of her carved sovereign effigies in her hands. The effigy stood atop a cresting curl of wave; it was Shirin, the sovereign of Tides, the patron of anyone with a Water Talent. "It smells a lie it smells a lie it smells a lie."

The water dripped louder—a leaky tap, a gutter overflowing, a line of tears trailing down a cheek. The effigy statue was crying. Its tears formed a pool around Mireille's feet, and the pool fed a stream, and the stream led to the well's dark maw.

They were in the wellhouse. How had they gotten here?

Rhia started to ask Mireille, but the earth choked her.

Somewhere nearby, a monster huffed. Its hot breath blew the hair off the back of her neck. The claws tapping became a frantic scrabbling against hard-packed dirt. No, it wasn't claws. It was her own fingers scraping at the dirt.

She was buried alive, drowning in dry earth.

Rhia screamed, and woke up to the sound of screaming.

It took her a moment to place herself. She lay in bed, the sun arcing cruelly into her eyes, and took a long moment just soothing her racing heart, drinking slow droughts of warm air into grateful lungs. The scream faded, a remnant of her dream.

She sat up, groggy, mouth tasting like an orchard full of rotting apple trees.

She didn't remember how she'd made it back to the house last night, but clearly she'd had a good time getting there. Her clothing was a trail from the door to the bed. One of her socks was still on. She was urgently, but not desperately, hung over.

Nothing a rasher of bacon, a loaf of toast, and a half-dozen eggs won't fix—

It took a moment to realize the second scream was not a lingering echo of her dream. It was a child, outside, not far away. It could be hard to tell the difference between a scream of joy and a scream of terror when a kid was doing it, but when the sound dissolved into bubbling sobs, Rhia levered herself out of bed and searched around for her boots.

There was a crowd down the street from Rhia's house, most of them clustered in the middle of the road. Every head pointed in the same direction. As Rhia approached, a young man broke out of the crowd, ran across the street, and threw up against the base of a porch.

Rhia approached the back of the crowd.

"What could've done it?" someone murmured.

"Never hurt a soul."

"—an accident?"

"His head's just, just—"

"—greyhowler—"

Will, the large soft-faced man from Columb, stood at the edge of the group. He was shaking his head, mopping his shiny pate with a kerchief. It was sweating-hot already.

Will nodded at Rhia. "Good morning, Courier. Gods, what a tragedy."

"What is it?" She asked, up on tiptoe, trying to see over the shoulders in front of her.

He was tall enough to see over most of the people, and his expression was grim. "A poor soul lost their life last night. An accident . . . it seems."

Rhia's stomach dropped. "It seems?"

The crowd burst apart as a small form pelted out from its center. A young teenager, face melted with tears, raced away down the street. Brown curls, pink shift, oversized sandals—the girl from yesterday morning. Sofie. Rensoa's sister.

No.

Rhia used the temporary opening left by Sofie's departure to snake through the crowd.

A long, skinny form measured its length on the dirt between two houses, partially in shadow. It was face-down, one hand stretched out over its head like it was beckoning for something. The back of the head was a red mass of chipped bone and dark, clotted hair.

Rhia swayed. She'd seen death before, but at a distance, or during a memorial, anointed and cleaned, handled respectfully. Not this. Not a real person with their head scrambled across the ground like a dropped basket of eggs.

Seeing the body as something that used to be a person turned him into one: the hair, the knobby limbs, the skinny shoulders, and too-big feet. The dark blue sweater she'd seen him wearing last night.

She fought against recognizing him. She didn't want to recognize him.

"Here now, give way." Micah was a sturdy presence at the back of the crowd. As they parted to let him through, the idea of someone in charge approaching was enough to let Rhia get steady on her feet and swallow back last night's dinner.

The headman settled in next to her and surveyed the scene. Dismay wrote itself across his face. "Ah, no. What's happened here?"

The crowd burbled up a dozen different explanations:

"Fell off the porch, hit his head—"

"—been drinking—"

"An argument, late in the night, I heard it—"

"The greyhowler—"

"The *greyhowler*—"

"Be easy!" Micah raised both hands, stilling the group. "Be easy. We can piece it together later. Let's get him indoors. Can't leave him laying here like this, it's not decent. Will—"

Rhia had been half-afraid he was going to ask her to pick up the corpse, given that she wasn't from Cerretour and was least likely to be affected by the death. She ceded her place to the big man with a sigh of relief.

"Gentle now—get his feet, you ready? Okay, up—"

The body sagged horribly as they lifted it , head drooping like a wilting tulip at the end of its stem. Gore spattered. The crowd pulsed back, revulsion visible on many faces.

"Clear out, you lot," Will said to the assembly, his tone softening the words. "There's nothing to do for him now."

"We need a house. Courier, you're in that one?" Micah tipped his chin in the direction of her borrowed house. "D'you mind? Mine's too far—"

"Go for it," Rhia said blankly, because she couldn't imagine saying anything else.

She shadowed the two men as they hurried down the street, corpse bobbing between them. Blood dripped a slapdash trail along the road.

"Lay him out on the floor," Micah gritted as Rhia darted ahead to open the door. The headman's face was ruddy, sweat raising on his brow.

"Sorry about the mess," she felt obliged to say as they carted the body inside. At this distance, the smell of blood was overwhelming. Her stomach contracted, tried to squeeze up into her throat.

"Micah, look at this." Will knelt beside the corpse's head, not visibly distressed by the proximity. He reached out with a fingertip and stirred a lock of black hair away from the cratered skull.

Rhia's stomach punched up into her throat and she swallowed hard. Something was embedded in the mass of tissue and blood, smooth and round among the jagged spokes of bone.

Micah leaned in. "What is—"

"It's a stone," Will said quietly. "Someone killed him with a stone."

He settled back on his heels, a series of conclusions chasing each other across his face. Rhia couldn't parse what any of them meant.

"*Luus shelter us from evil,*" Will murmured, prompting an automatic "*And valor light our way*" from Rhia. Because she was already looking at him, it was impossible to miss his surprise as she finished the prayer. She was surprised too: most people knew scripture well enough to quote it like he had last night, but an invocation of the gods was usually only spoken by clergy. They looked askance at each other.

"This couldn't have been an accident," Micah continued, not noticing their confusion. "Not and have him end up facedown like that. Someone hit him in the back of the head. Let's get him turned over."

The corpse's face was swollen and dark with displaced blood, but unmistakably Rensoa. The mouth had pulled up in a sneer that was nearly the one he'd given her last night when he bid her farewell. One of his eyes was open. Light smeared across its dry surface, rather than catching in a single wet point, and that more than anything else made the immediacy of his death impossible to ignore.

Rhia excused herself and barely made it out the front door before she lost it. Everything came up—cider and chicken and wrinkly grapes, search parties and celebrations and nightmares and water gurgling up into the well, so intense that by the end of it spots danced in front of her eyes. She caught her breath, hands on her knees, and told herself that the tears on her face were from exertion, not emotion.

He's just a kid. Was. *Someone killed him, and he was just a kid.* She gulped in air.

When she got back to the house, Micah had taken the sheet off the bed and they were winding the corpse in it.

"I'll have to tell his folks," the headman was saying.

"Not if his sister's gotten there first," Will said.

"I'll go myself regardless. It's respectful. I should tell them."

"And Creff," Rhia said, remembering the tenderness with which the older man had touched Rensoa's shoulder two afternoons ago, out there on the prairie.

The two men looked up, startled, like they'd forgotten she was there.

"Aye. And Creff." Micah levered himself up to his feet. "We'll hold a service. Mireille can do it. I haven't seen her this morning. If either of you do, will you have her find me?"

"Aye."

"Sure."

"We should . . . *I* should lay him out in the front room at my house. That feels . . . more appropriate." Micah looked at Rhia and Will, as if asking for permission, and she realized regardless of his assertive language, Micah was as disturbed by all this as she was.

"His people would appreciate that," Will agreed. He must have come to the same conclusion. His face was full of compassion.

Micah nodded. "Then help me with him."

It took the three of them together to lift Rensoa's body off the ground and into Micah's arms. Buffered by the intermediary of the shroud, picking up the corpse was less creepy than she feared. *Easy to pretend it's just an awkward package for delivery*, she thought, and the thought made her terribly sad.

Micah cradled the body like an oversized baby. Rhia and Will watched from the doorway as he lumbered slowly down the street, his ponderous gait lending a processional air to his movement. A funeral train of one.

Rhia thought of Rensoa. All of her experiences with him were filled with his anger. Last night at the celebration, under the tree yesterday morning, and out on the prairie the day before. He'd been so certain, so indignant. It had been easy to label that intensity as teenage passion and nothing more—but now that there wouldn't be anything more from Rensoa, Rhia regretted she hadn't done more to connect with him. She remembered the bones of his face carved out by lanternlight last night, the hot points of his eyes. His pain—his frustration—had been real. He had died thinking no one cared enough to listen to him.

"Fuck, this is awful." She pinched the bridge of her nose. The hangover, poor sleep, and empty stomach were all catching up to her at once.

"It's not given to us to know how our stories end," Will said. "I only hope it was fast and painless, and that he's resting now in the fields with his ancestors."

Rhia shook her head. Her patience for faith-talk was in even shorter supply than usual. The gods always seemed to have plenty to say in comfort after terrible shit happened and nothing to say to prevent it.

"You look skeptical, but you knew the end of Luus' invocation." Will looked at her with soft brown eyes. "It's not just that you trained in the Temple, is it? You lived there. You were an acolyte. The holy ways aren't new to you."

"Or to you, I noticed."

"Aye." He grimaced. "Courier, I'm afraid that last night, I wasn't completely candid about why I'm—"

"Micah!"

A teenager sprinted up the street. He stopped on the path up to the house, bent over with his hands on his knees. "Need—Micah!"

"You just missed him," Rhia said.

"What's going on, child?" Will asked.

"The well!" He gasped for air. "The well. It's dry again."

An hour later, Micah, Priano, and Rhia clustered in the wellhouse, looking into the empty stone-lined puncture.

Being in the wellhouse placed her squarely back in the nightmare. Over and over, her eyes drifted into the well. The opening was opaque, velvety black. She kept imagining someone looking out. Did she hear water dripping? *Be easy, Rhia. Steady as she goes.*

Priano was crying. Just a little, trying to keep it together, but clearly distraught. "We'll have to keep going," he was saying. "Gather up the whole town, even them as won't want to listen, and move us all somewhere greener. Somewhere safe."

Micah's brow was furrowed so deeply Rhia could barely see his eyes. He scrubbed his palm over his face. He looked exhausted, frustrated, but he spoke with calm authority.

"Bear up, everyone. First thing is to inventory what casks are left from our trip. Should be most of them, and there's a spot of luck: people spent a lot of time yesterday afternoon filling up their jugs and buckets from the well." He smiled wanly. It came across as more of a wince. "That will stay us for a time." His gaze lifted up to Rhia. "Courier, I hate to impose again . . ."

"It's no trouble." It was, actually; she was sad and hung over and trying hard not to let the memory of her nightmare infect the present. But none of that mattered at the moment.

Rhia sat down, her back pressed against the well's stone wall. Spurred on by her anxiety, her Talent woke quickly and plunged deep down the wellshaft, eager as a scenting hound.

The aquifer rested deep underground, fresh and rich. That little pool of groundwater lay trapped in its pocket near the surface. Everything was as it had been the day before, but this time, when Rhia summoned the water, it wouldn't come. She cajoled and pulled and demanded until a spike of pain shot through her head, and it just. Wouldn't. Come.

"What's it doing?" Micah stood close enough to the well that his voice boomed and echoed back.

Rhia blinked back into her body, sweating. For an instant, the gloom of the wellhouse became the dry darkness of her nightmare.

"I—I'm not sure. It's there, but I . . . I can't bring it up today."

The admission itself was frightening. She was a seventh-degree Talent. Water never disobeyed her. She felt weak-handed, helpless, a strong swimmer adrift at sea.

"This town is cursed," Priano whispered. "The greyhowler takes it all."

"Keep your heart up," Micah squeezed his husband's shoulder, but Rhia could see he was as worried as the rest of them. "Mayhap we overdrew from it yesterday and by tomorrow, it'll be full again. We'll figure something out . . ."

His gaze fell on the door, and Rhia imagined what lay beyond it—the parching heat, the weeping family, the memorial.

"Thank you for trying, Courier. I'm sure you'll want to be on your way, but you're welcome to stay for the service, if you like."

"I would," she said, surprising herself.

"Thank you." Micah boosted her to her feet and gestured them both back out into the sun, the heat, the inexorably progressing day. "We have a funeral to plan. We must speak with Mireille."

They did not find the acolyte in Cerretour.

It was a small town; there weren't that many places to look. She wasn't in the streets chasing children, or under the shade of a porch telling them stories. She wasn't walking in the farm fields. She wasn't sitting with Rensoa's family in their grief. The potting sheds were empty except for the exhausted potato plants, collapsing in their pots.

Rhia searched all these places and then searched them again, worry kindling in her heart. Rensoa was dead. Tansin, still missing. An animal stalked the streets at night. Something was happening in Cerretour, and now Mireille might be caught in it.

Rhia waited to check the acolyte's house until last, because if Mireille wasn't there, she would have nowhere else to look.

People lingered in the street, talking quietly. Someone wept. Someone else had hung a woven prayer chain between two houses. It stirred in the breeze. The dust in the air had already dulled the fabric's bright colors; deep violet, sunny yellow, cloud grey. Whoever had hung the prayer chain had made their finest offering with it. The spot where they'd hung it was where Rensoa's body had been found, Rhia realized.

Purple, gold, and silver: Temple colors, rich folks' colors, the colors of the ribbon on the letter she'd delivered to Micah.

"Courier, take an amulet," A middle-aged woman offered her a folded square of purple fabric.

"A what?" Rhia examined the palm-sized object. It was a fabric sachet, crudely stitched shut with white and yellow thread. Given how it smelled, there were herbs inside.

"For your safety. All the women in town are making them." When Rhia's face indicated no change in comprehension, the woman continued: "It'll protect you from the greyhowler."

"Oh for—" Fatigue and frustration combined into something treacherous and she bit her tongue on a very rude reply. "Ma'am, the greyhowler isn't real."

"How can you say that?" The woman asked, stung. "When it was here? It killed our own Rensoa!"

"I'm sorry," Rhia said. "I'm very sorry. But please—this town's imagination is running wild. This monster—has anyone ever even seen it?"

"Mireille said," the woman insisted. "Mireille told us the greyhowler comes at night."

Rhia couldn't bring herself to argue any more with this woman who was scared and grieving and trying to make sense of a senseless thing. She shoved the amulet in her pocket and strode away.

Mireille's house was empty.

The sounds of the people in the street outside crowded against her ears. Rhia hovered in the doorway, torn between respecting Mireille's privacy and avoiding more conversations with frightened, superstitious people.

The effigies on the altar were watching her.

She went inside.

The air inside the house was dull, undisturbed by recent activity. All Mireille's possessions lay as they had when Rhia had been here three days ago. The bed was made. The little altar was neatly arranged, down to the ceramic bowl of flower petals Mireille had knocked out of place and caught with her Talent. A line of ash sat in the bottom of an incense tray. Rhia pressed a finger to it. *Cold.*

"Find anything?" Will's broad shoulders blocked most of the light coming in through the doorway.

Rhia jumped, guilty as a thief, and shook her head. Her lower lip was numb from biting.

Will crossed the threshold, stood next to her before the altar. He looked down at it with a precise and specific interest. He bent and picked up a carved effigy from the altar. Artis, Sovereign of Gales, the patron of Air Talents. The god was usually depicted standing on a pile of books and scrolls, surrounded by birds, face turned to the sky. This figure stood on a crude wooden mound, books represented by chopped lines, birds absent. His facial features were marked by simple slits.

"This is, hmm, amateurish, isn't it? Carved by hand, I'd say."

"I guess." Rhia shrugged. "I'm not from around here. I figured it was a local thing, making your own figures."

"I should say not." He placed the figure back on the altar with a reverence that belied his critique, pressed a thumb into the incense ash and touched it to his lips. The gesture stirred Rhia's memory.

"Rensoa's family wishes to see him buried before sundown," he murmured. His voice was distant. He could have been remarking on the weather. "They seemed quite insistent."

"They're worried about the greyhowler." Rhia remembered Sofie's terrified insistence that Rensoa stay within the town limits, that if he went out on the prairie he'd fall prey to the monster. The memory hurt. "It comes out at night. That's what they believe, I mean. They believe it eats the dead."

"Ghastly." Faint distaste wrinkled Will's brow.

"If Mireille's not back by then . . ." Rhia shook her head. "They'll be at peace with a secular service, won't they? Cerretour doesn't usually have a Priest to do the full rites."

"That's of no concern. I can do the rites."

Rhia peered at him. "You what?"

"I was going to tell you back in your house, when we were—after Micah had taken Rensoa to his family. I'm a Priest."

This soft-eyed, approachable man was about as far from the Priests of her memory as she could imagine. Rhia gaped. "No you're—a Priest? But—you're not in robes. You, you look like a regular person. You were digging up *pipes* yesterday, for gods' sakes!"

He smiled sheepishly. "I know. I know. I'm here . . . incognito."

She ran back through her encounters with Will over the last two days and a half-dozen oddities aligned with each other. His propensity for dropping lines of scripture into conversation. His abstinence from drinking at the party. The soft, uncalloused hands that clashed with his overall musculature. The ease with which he'd wound Rensoa's body into a sheet, which suggested a firsthand familiarity with the rituals of death. The way he'd recited Luus' invocation, speaking it as reflexively as she had. And here, in this room, the tenderness with which he'd handled the effigy at Mireille's altar, the way he'd kissed his ash-smeared thumb.

She frowned. Yesterday, on the walk from the wellhouse to the spring, she'd felt comforted by his presence. It had felt good to know she wasn't the only one who didn't believe in the greyhowler. She'd been grateful to know she wasn't alone.

Grateful. She seethed. *I was honest with him. I was open. And he lied right to my face.*

Will was still talking. "The type of work I do for the Temple . . . it mandates a degree of secrecy. I'm sorry I wasn't more forthcoming earlier. I wouldn't have said anything at all if I hadn't realized you were Temple-raised as well."

"What's that got to do with anything?"

"I think you might understand the sensitivity of the situation. This isn't a good time for someone to go missing."

"When is it ever a good time?"

"Now especially, I mean. Someone dies unexpectedly in the night, likely at the hands of another, and then someone else disappears. It doesn't look innocent, does it?"

Rhia felt her mouth open. A pool of silence spread between them.

"He was found not two doors down from this very house," Will pointed out.

"How dare." Rhia was aghast. Heat bled up from her hands and into her face. "How *dare* you accuse Mireille of something like that."

"I'm not accusing anyone of anything," Will said mildly. "I'm drawing what I believe to be a fairly obvious connection."

"Mireille cared about Rensoa. He wanted to go searching for Tansin out on the prairie and she stopped him. She cares about everyone here! She's busted her ass for this town since the drought started. I've seen it. She wants everyone to be safe."

"She's been here for over a month, Courier. A long stop, for an acolyte on her roving. You grew up in the Temple. You know that's odd. Doesn't that seem odd to you?"

"No! I don't know. No. There's a drought! What's she supposed to do? You—you walk in here, lie to folks about who you are, and accuse someone like that, like her, of murder? You don't even know her."

"Do you?"

The intensity of his eyes on her face was unbearable. Rhia took a step back from him, and when that wasn't enough, put herself in the doorway.

"Better than you do, surely. And I know you too. You're a *Priest*." She could hear the spite in her voice and didn't care to soften it. "The second a Priest sees something that won't fit their mold, all they want is to break it down so it will."

Distress and hurt flashed over his face. "I'm not here to break anything, Rhia. You should know that. I'm about the gods' business. If you hadn't left the Temple, you could very well be doing the same. And if you were, you'd understand that I'm only here to help."

"Yeah, that's what people like you always say. You think you know better than everyone. You want to *help*, Priest? Do something useful. Find Mireille. And in the meantime, stay the fuck away from me." Rhia spun on her heel and strode out into the sun.

She let fury carry her past the impromptu memorial hung between the houses, through a crowd of murmuring townspeople, and down the street. She was so angry her fingers were snapping. The street ran out before her energy did and she marched out into the prairie. Tall grass whisked around her thighs. A ground squirrel darted out from under her pounding feet, shimmied its narrow body through the undergrowth to escape.

In that moment, Will Cordance was every Priest at Roundtree Temple who had turned their back on her, every stride away from him was a stride away from the home that had rejected her.

Rhia broke through the edge of the grass and found herself at the edge of the dry spring. Her ears were ringing. She took a deep breath, trying to slow her heart rate, and then another.

She knew some of her anger was leftover from her past. It felt too familiar, a daughter of the Temple doing what she perceived to be her duty, only to be rejected and maligned by the senior members of the faith.

He's treating Mireille just like they treated me.

Rhia kicked a stone at the edge of the dry spring and watched it shoot over the prairie grass. She imagined it hitting the ground, the thump and thatchy crush of grass. She imagined how the stone that killed him had embedded itself in Rensoa's skull. She couldn't imagine how hard someone would have had to throw it, to sink it in so deeply.

In her mind's eye, the ceramic bowl tumbled from the altar. Mireille's Talent caught it in midair and floated it back up to rest on the table. Unbidden, Rhia's imagination extended the memory—the bowl shot toward her face, fast and inescapable as a meteor. Impact, with a sound of broken pottery; the bowl, or her skull, or both.

No.

A plains bird called from the brush, a low, liquid, rippling sound. The well, filling with a sound like sobbing. Her Talent had filled the well. Tansin had been the town's only Water Talent. Tansin, who had gone missing a few weeks after Mireille arrived in Cerretour. Tansin, who wanted nothing more in the world than to be a Priest. Tansin, who Rensoa had said was Mireille's friend, but Mireille had said she didn't know well.

There was something just off the edge of the map in her mind, a landmark that, once it came clearly into view, would become a waypoint by which she could orient herself.

The dusty blue horizon loomed in every direction.

She did not want to look.

Rhia turned and stared back into Cerretour. She was far enough out of town that she could see people moving along the road, between the buildings, but they couldn't see her. Maybe Mireille had come back. Either way, they would be making ready for the funeral.

She couldn't stop herself from imagining Sophie running away from the body. Her memory flashed to the night of her arrival, the nameless woman weeping on the porch as the search party came in from the prairie.

Priano, standing by the well, crying quietly and trying to hide it. Everyone in Cerretour had reason to weep.

So much has happened to this town. These people don't deserve any of this.

The bird called again, drawing her attention. Behind her, the prairie was unchanged.

She walked away from it, from the dry spring and the stones and the sweeping empty face of the continent, back to Cerretour and the things she already knew.

Rhia sweated through her uniform jacket before the procession bearing Rensoa's wrapped body arrived at the little graveyard outside of town. Someone had dug a grave, and there were small piles of earth and stones laid out beside it. Burying someone in Cerretour was a community affair, Rhia understood. Everyone was expected to participate, even the Courier, new in town and still a stranger to most of them.

Maybe this is just what funerals are like in places like this, she thought as the pallbearers came into view. *Everyone knows everyone, everyone gathers to say goodbye. Birth to death, people spend their lives in just one place.*

"*Their ancestors are buried here,*" Mireille had said.

Standing clumped in the larger group of mourners, Rhia felt as far away from them as she had on the prairie. She didn't know her ancestors. She had come to the Temple as an orphan. And if her foster-family counted as ancestry, well, she was still far from home.

Home. She hadn't thought of the Temple in that context in years, had deliberately broken herself of the habit. Now, as the funeral procession grew closer, her palms grew clammy and a lump swelled in her throat. She told herself it was the emotion intrinsic to a funeral. She told herself it was the heat.

If I died tomorrow, who would bury me?

She swallowed the lump, shoved the question to the back of her mind, and focused on the funeral.

The pallbearers were two men, a woman, and a person of indeterminate gender. Rensoa's family, probably. They lowered the body into the narrow grave on a sheet, and let the edges drape over it, obscuring the point of nose, A curl of black hair escaped from the shroud. They settled the board on which he'd been carried on top of the corpse like a lid. No one laid flowers. There were no flowers to be had.

Someone was weeping softly. It could have been any one of the mourners. It could have been all of them.

The sun was still a comforting number of fingers above the horizon, but it didn't stop people from looking out into the prairie as Will intoned prayers. Heat waves rippled and collapsed in the grass.

Time passed. The sun wrung the emotion out of Rhia. She stood half-listening, wondering if Rensoa would even have noticed that she'd dressed in full uniform for his funeral, or if she'd pass out from heat exhaustion before they even got to the songs.

Will had produced a set of robes from somewhere, and in the summer sun the undyed linen was almost too bright to look at directly. He really was a Priest, she noted with some chagrin; he knew all the rites and all the prayers. His face was set in a perpetual smear of grim, ceremonial sadness. When he moved his hands to emphasize a phrase, or to invoke a ritual gesture, the gold and silver thread embroidering his cuffs flashed in the sun. Gold and silver. Priest colors. She thought again of the letter she'd come to Cerretour to deliver. Had it only been three days? Three days felt like weeks ago. The heat was making her a little dizzy.

There was still no sign of Mireille.

When the service concluded, Rhia stood in line to assist with the burial. Most people chose to throw a shovel of dirt over the board. The piles of stones lay untouched, perhaps out of sensitivity to how Rensoa had died.

The grave filled rapidly. Rhia chose a rock and knelt to lay it on the growing mound.

"I'm sorry this happened to you, kid," she whispered. She pressed the stone into the dry earth.

The funeral concluded as the sun's bottom curve brushed the horizon. Everyone walked back to town awash in sundown light the color of blood. An enormous gibbous moon blossomed up from the other side of the sky.

There would be no wake. Last night's frenzied, joyous mood had snuffed out completely replaced by a subdued, grim atmosphere not unlike the one that had hung over the town the night Rhia had arrived.

"Courier Silver."

Micah and Priano waited on the side of the road just outside of town. Each man wore a fine-woven shirt and vest. The creases pressed into them told her they were usually stored in chests and brought out once or twice a year.

They were both looking expectantly at her. Rhia pulled out of the crowd and stopped next to them.

"Evening," she said, and then, because it felt polite: "That was a lovely service."

"Aye." Micah scratched the back of his neck, tugged on his shirt collar. "Thank you for attending."

"It was the least I could do."

"Very fortunate that Will was here. It's the right thing, having a Priest conduct a funeral. It doesn't feel as sacred, when we do our own."

"What a blessing," Rhia deadpanned. Priano picked up on her sarcasm, but Micah missed it. He looked worn out.

"That he is. It's not often you meet a Priest traveling like that. When we met in Columb, he told me he'd been all over the province, ministering to different towns. Pure luck that we ran into him when we did; more so that he asked to come back with us."

"Hard to call any of this *lucky*," Priano murmured.

"Aye, there's that." Micah made an expression that was less smile, more wince. "You still haven't seen Mireille, I take it?"

Rhia frowned. "No. You haven't either?"

"No . . . I wanted to speak to you, Courier—about the letter you brought me."

"My delivery? Sure."

"You didn't happen to speak with anyone about it, did you? Before you gave it to me."

"Speak to . . . what do you mean?" Rhia paged back through her memory. "I don't think so? I mean, not beyond what's obvious. I'm a Courier. Everyone who recognizes the uniform knows I've come to a place to deliver something or take something away."

"Then you didn't read the letter yourself?"

"Of course not," she said, a little offended. "I never do. That's part of the job." She frowned. There was something on Micah's face she didn't like. "Is there something you'd like to ask me directly, headman?"

"Oh, no." Micah's lips flattened against each other. "This afternoon, I finally had time to open it. It's from the Head Priest of Bywater Temple."

She'd been right about the letter being sealed with Temple colors, then. Bywater was a Temple about twenty miles northeast of Tellemont, at the root of the river Telles. Rhia knew of it, but had never visited. She imagined the wax seal popping, the ribbon slithering purple and silver and gold across Micah's desk.

What would the Temple have to say to a village headman? What would they have to say that was urgent enough to send a Courier—that required a Courier's level of discretion and privacy?

"From how it's written, I reckon every village head and mayor within ten leagues has received a letter just like it." Micah continued. "It cast a new light—and one I don't much like—on some of the things that have happened in town recently."

"Which things?"

He shook his head. "Just . . . if you see Mireille? Please come find me right away."

He and Priano bid her goodnight and joined the people on the road going back into town. As they walked, Micah's head drooped suddenly, like the muscles in his neck could no longer withstand an incalculable weight. Priano put a comforting hand in the center of his husband's back.

Rhia watched, nonplussed, until the roads ran empty.

Back in her house, she pulled off her uniform and stood in the center of the room in her underwear. Sweat steamed. She saturated a bandanna with water from a basin and gave herself a quick bath. Afterward, she dressed in clean trousers and shirt.

She ought to be packing. She could leave as early as the next morning. There would be more deliveries, more destinations, once she was back in Tellemont. She used the idea of it—the city on the hill, rolling tawny cobblestones, the iron gaslamps lighting the streets at night, the sweeping elms, the river running crystal in the open canals—as a goad that got her halfway through loading her pack before her eye fell on the dark smear of Rensoa's blood on the floor and her motivation sputtered out.

The bed creaked as it accepted her weight. The prairie grass sighed in the darkness outside. She hadn't heard the greyhowler tonight, she realized. Maybe it had finally moved on.

Maybe it was in the graveyard eating Rensoa's corpse.

She shook her head. *That's horrible.*

The mouth of her half-empty pack hung slack. She couldn't bring herself to fill it.

Rensoa was dead. Mireille was missing. Soon the town would be as dry as it had been when Rhia arrived. She had delivered her message. There was no point in staying longer. It was time to go.

Wasn't it?

Her head ached dully. She was thirsty. She gulped from her waterskin. When she put it back on the table, her fingers brushed against the crumpled fabric of the amulet the woman had given her that afternoon.

She paused. It was a stupid superstition to protect from a made-up monster, but it was also heartfelt. A weak gesture of hope from people who had lost so much.

She had gotten so accustomed to only thinking of herself.

In her memory, Will said *I'm about the gods' business. If you hadn't left the Temple, you could very well be doing the same.*

She hated the idea of meeting his expectations . . . but if there was a way she could help, didn't she have to try?

I can't just leave.

I should try the well again. Just once. Just to see if . . .

It felt stupid to hope. The aquifer had been as immovable as a glacier when she'd tried to bring the water up this morning. When she noticed her own self-doubt, it made her angry, and she latched onto that. The idea of not leaving when she had the opportunity was so at odds with her perception of herself, she didn't know what to do with it . . . but anger was fuel, and fuel, she could use.

Rhia went out into the street.

She stalked through the night, sticking to the shadows. The nearly-full moon cast an unrelenting silvery light. Rhia was grateful for the black clothing that rendered her invisible to anyone who might have looked out their windows. She didn't want to meet anyone out here tonight, didn't want to explain what was undoubtedly a fool's errand.

Rhia was barely out beyond the last buildings when she saw Mireille.

Moonlight made the acolyte's robes into a smear of cream against the parched silver and speckled grey of the prairie grass. She was rushing up the road in the same direction Rhia was headed. Into the prairie. Toward the wellhouse.

Rhia opened her mouth to call out . . . and shut it again.

If there was a connection between Mireille's absence, Will's accusation, Micah's suspicion, and Rensoa's death, Rhia wanted to understand it before she spoke to anyone else. Including Mireille.

Silently, she followed the acolyte down the road.

The path to the wellhouse hit the main road at a perpendicular angle. Mireille paused at the intersection for a moment, as if gathering her thoughts, then continued toward the building.

As Rhia turned onto the path, she noticed a fresh set of those swooping marks smeared into the dust. Mireille's robes must have left them as they swished back and forth.

She's been coming out here every day. What's she been doing?

Mireille let herself into the wellhouse and Rhia increased her pace to a jog. Micah's instructions to find him immediately if she saw Mireille were barely a whisper in the back of her mind. Her curiosity was overwhelming. Micah could wait.

Rhia approached the welhouse. On one side of the path, the length of pipe Will had dug up yesterday lay exposed, a straight dark line in the earth. On the other side, the short length of vent pipe punctured the ground. As Rhia got closer, she heard something. It was a whispering murmur that brought her back to the last time she'd been alone in the wellhouse, when she'd heard something that might have been a voice. She followed the sound off the path, to the vertical vent pipe.

She knelt down outside the wellhouse door next to the vent pipe. A stutter of rippling sound came from it.

It was a voice coming from underground.

"... secret ...

"... help us ..."

A woman's voice. Distorted by the metal, and at such a low volume, it was impossible to identify, but it must have been Mireille. Who else could it be?

Rhia sat back on her heels, confused. How was Mireille's voice coming from underground?

A line of pulsing, leaf-green light bled under the wellhouse door. Mireille was using her Talent.

Rhia stood up, brushed her hands off, and went inside.

A lantern hung from a nail on a wall beam. Mireille knelt beside the well, silhouetted by fluttering green light. A column of earth was lifting off the ground in front of her like a cork being drawn out of a wine bottle.

When Mireille heard the door open, the light went out. The pile of dirt plopped unceremoniously back onto the ground.

"Rhia?" Mireille blinked sleepily through the disorientation that came from suddenly reentering your own body. "What are you doing here?"

"I could ask the same of you," Rhia said as she shut the door behind her. "Nobody's seen you all day."

Mireille brushed dirty hands off on her robes. "I've been out on the prairie since dawn. I was looking for water."

The air in the wellhouse hung heavy and thick. Rhia felt that same sense of dread, of inevitability, she had felt every time she came in here. It was so consistent she had felt it in her nightmare.

Now Mireille was here too. Just like her nightmare.

"People were worried about you, Mireille. Micah has been looking for you."

"I'm so sorry," Mireille said. "First thing tomorrow, I'll find him and tell him I'm all right. But what brings you out here at this hour?"

What brings you out here?

A half-dozen facts rattled together like loose stones in her mind. Stones. The ceramic bowl. The pillar of earth, shivering out of the ground.

"I gave Micah the letter I carried. By all rights, I should have left Cerretour this morning. But I wanted to stay for the funeral. I figured if I'm here another night, I couldn't rest easy without trying to unblock the well one more time."

"The well is dry, Rhia. What could there be to find?"

There was an odd tension in Mireille's voice.

"Mireille," Rhia said quietly. "Aren't you going to ask me whose funeral it was?"

The acolyte's face went the same color as her robes.

"What?"

When Will had raised the possibility, it had made her angry. She'd felt defensive of Mireille. She hadn't wanted to believe it.

Rhia articulated her next words carefully: "You were out on the prairie since dawn, you said. You shouldn't even know that someone died."

She took a long step forward, putting herself beside the well. She was within three feet of the other woman now.

"Mireille, did you kill Rensoa?"

A sob burst out of Mireille, propelled out of her lungs like an escaping bird. It echoed. She covered her mouth.

"It was an accident. It was an accident. I'm sorry. I didn't mean to—He was shouting at me. I—I got afraid."

Using your Talent to work violence against another person was blasphemy. The taboo had been engrained in her in childhood. The room swam. Rhia swayed, put her hand on the side of the well.

"Oh, Mireille," she said.

The acolyte made a sharp gesture of denial. "I can explain. He found me last night. In the street. Confronted me. He said there must be some reason I was so invested in keeping everyone here, in making folks stay. He said I didn't want folks looking for Tansin anymore, and if I was out after dark, I must be making the sounds everyone heard at night, trying to keep folks indoors. He said that I was the greyhowler. He said he was going to get Micah. I . . . panicked."

"Why?" Rhia asked. "Micah would have talked some sense into the kid . . . right?"

Mireille's chin wobbled. "I was afraid."

"Afraid of what?"

Her voice dropped to a whisper. "I was afraid he'd read your letter."

"Why would you—wait a minute, it was you? Did you break into my house?"

Things were coming together too quickly to make sense. She didn't know what was going on. A story was creating itself in the ocean of her mind, coming into view like a whale surfacing underneath a fishing boat.

Adrenaline made her veins into wires of white-hot metal, clearing her vision, sharpening her thoughts. Her Talent uncoiled, responding to her agitation. It reacted: there was water nearby. That wasn't unexpected—the aquifer was still down below the well, quiet and deep.

But there was also something else.

Rhia found herself walking. Her hands were out from her sides and she swayed gently back and forth; a dowser's walk, a water-finder's walk.

She came to a halt standing on the loose earth that had been Mireille's dirt column. Beneath it, the little patch of groundwater she had felt earlier that day, and yesterday.

It had been there the whole time. She just hadn't paid attention to it.

"Rhia—" Mireille's voice spiraled up and cracked.

Rhia dropped to her knees and began to pull at the dirt floor. It was soft and came up easily. The earth had recently been turned.

"Rhia, wait—"

She was on the scent now and wouldn't be stopped. Rhia immersed both arms halfway to the elbow. Whatever she was sensing, it was farther down than she could reach. She sat back on her heels, put her Talent into the water, and *pulled*.

It felt different. She knew about aquifers contained deep in the earth and riverheads seeping out of mountains and rain lowering in heavy-bottomed clouds and the ethereal promise of moisture suspended in mist. This body of water felt different, loosely contained in one spot, stagnant, barely seeping out into the ground around it, not the pure water of stone-filtered springs or condensing rainclouds, but pungent, acrid, laced with rot—

The earth softened under her knees.

Rhia snatched her hands off the ground. They came away muddy. The ground in front of her was wet.

A bubble of water pulsed up from underground and into the wellhouse, carrying with it the scent of waste and stale air.

Buoyed up on the swell of filthy water, a coil of dark lines webbed together. They were half-buried in the earth still, a promise of continuation beneath. Long, dark loops, twining through the pool like kelp. Hair.

Rhia had already seen death once today, discovered, examined, and buried it. She didn't have it in her to feel shocked or disgusted anymore.

She plunged her hand back down into the earth, using a dab of Talent to moisten the dirt and ease the way. Her fingers became eyes, mapped a figure as she pressed further down, burying her arm past the elbow. They stumbled across a cheekbone, smeared over lips, bounced off a collarbone. She found a shoulder. Beside it, as if reaching for someone, a hand.

Rhia brushed her fingers against the stranger's.

"There's a body—" she gasped over her shoulder. "Someone's buried here, by the well—"

Mireille made a high-pitched, wavery noise, the sound of glass vibrating its way up to shattering.

Deep beneath the loose, wet soil, cold fingers clutched around Rhia's.

She shrieked, recoiling back, but her hand was caught tight. She was trapped in the ground, clutched by an unseen corpse. Rhia panicked. She pulled harder, bracing against the ground with her knees. Her shoulder popped. The ground squelched. She couldn't get free. She was sinking.

Her Talent surged with the raw and primal urge to escape. Fetid water burst up through the soft earth and spattered against the ceiling.

Suddenly her arm was moving. Her hand was still caught, so Rhia leaned back and hauled against the weight underground. She was pretty sure she was still screaming, but she couldn't be certain, because what was coming out of the earth demanded her full attention. Her elbow came up, then her hand, horribly clutched in the white knuckled-grip of another. A bare arm extended out of the earth. Next, the curve of brow and eye socket, a line of lip crusted with dirt, a face uptilted toward the roof. The mouth, pink and gaping. Chin. Shoulders, breasts, ribcage. Rhia was on her feet now, hauling with both hands.

She disinterred the woman in a gasp of liquid and stale air.

Rhia found herself on the ground, chest heaving. She cleared her throat and swallowed. Someone was still gasping. It was the woman, she realized. They were next to each other, breathing in unison.

She sat up, swayed with dizziness.

They were at the edge of a deep depression in the floor. Just beyond Rhia's boots, the ground gave way to an empty space. It was about ten feet by six feet across, set deep into the ground beneath the wellhouse. Water dripped down out of the puddle Rhia had made and plinked on the flat stone floor. Light glinted on a pipe jutting out of one packed earth wall.

Air. They made sure she had air.

As she watched, a section of the cell's wall, because that's what it was, a cell, a cell hidden under the wellhouse, cracked and crumbled onto the stone. Whatever Talent had kept it in place had evaporated away. Rhia tried to imagine being down there, trapped in the dark in a tiny space kept intact only by someone else's attention, and shuddered.

The woman's breath was reedy, wheezing. She had probably inhaled some dirt on her way up. She coughed twice, licked her lips and made a face of obvious distaste. She wore a light sleeveless dress, a woodprint of small flowers visible beneath the oily stains of dirt and waste. It was the kind you'd wear out in the garden or during a morning walk. This woman had been buried alive in it.

She was here. She was here the entire time.

A collection of water droplets picked themselves out of the thin puddle in which the woman lay, each one so clear and clean it was almost invisible. They darted through the air and swiped themselves across the woman's lips. She licked them away and sighed in relief.

"Tansin," Rhia said.

The woman's eyes opened and met hers.

"Thank you," she husked. Her voice was raw and gritty from disuse. She was still holding Rhia's hand. She squeezed it once and fell still.

Mireille made a strangled sound. Rhia had forgotten she was there. She did a quick assessment of her own strength and decided she could stand up. It took two tries.

When her vision straightened, she saw the expression on Mireille's face and a horrible new reality locked into place.

"You knew."

Mireille's eyes brimmed with tears. She nodded, her jaw shaking, looking like a puppet being operated at the end of very long sticks.

"Mireille, who—"

"She wanted to go with me," the acolyte whispered. "She wanted me to take her with me, when I left the town. She wanted to go to the Temple. It was all she would talk about. She wanted to be a Priest."

"So you, you—you put her in the *ground*?" Rhia's voice cracked on the way up. She was too close to the hole, all of a sudden, and took a big step away from it, as if it might swallow her just from proximity.

"I didn't mean to. Not forever, I mean. It was just supposed to be temporary."

Rhia didn't have words.

"I wasn't going to keep her here, I swear! It's just—she said she was going to go to a Temple, and I knew she wasn't strong enough to pass the trials and, and—I couldn't leave! They *needed* me!" The look on Mireille's face showed she knew she wasn't winning Rhia over. "It's not like I abandoned her! I was out here every day; I brought food, water—I kept her company! I would never just *leave* her—"

"But *why*?" Rhia shouted. "She wants to go with you to a Temple, okay, you know she's not going to be a Priest, okay, just—just tell her it's hopeless, or even, fuck, take her with you! The worst that happens is she gets to a Temple with you and they turn her away—"

Mireille's jaw muscles worked. She shook her head stiffly. "I thought . . . I thought if put her there long enough, maybe her Talent would . . . I thought she might get stronger. And then she could go, and I could stay! She could be a Priest! Just like she wanted."

"You were *tempering* her?" Rhia said. On the ground, Tansin emitted a little sob, as if the word itself carried pain. "Gods protect me, Mireille, that's—that's barbaric. It's *forbidden*, you told me yourself—"

Tansin groaned something from the floor. Swiftly, Rhia knelt down next to her. She was saying something.

"Not—she's not—not a real Priest."

"I know she's not. She's an acoly—"

But when Rhia looked up at Mireille, she realized she actually didn't know anything at all.

The little idea-stones in her mind were falling together into a shape, and the shape was a mound, it was a mountain, it was the landmark she hadn't wanted to look at directly this afternoon on the prairie, a thousand years ago.

Mireille's altar table, the effigies handmade.

Creff, blithely admitting he didn't know which Temple Mireille had come from.

The woman with the amulets, insisting the greyhowler was real, not because she had seen it but because Mireille had said it was.

Mireille, the very night Rhia had arrived in Cerretour, making sure she hadn't come from the Citadel.

The lusus mendace walks the earth at night hunting those who tell lies.

She's not a real Priest.

It occurred to Rhia that perhaps she should have been afraid. But there wasn't room for that. Instead she was terribly, terribly sad.

"Is this what you meant?" Rhia asked. Her voice broke on the question. "When you said *everything will work out the way it's supposed to?*"

"You don't understand, I was on the road for so long. I thought, if I went far enough away, I could do it. I could be a Priest. I could be someone else. I wandered for so long. But I was only ever me. And then I got here."

Mireille met Rhia's eyes for the first time and the guilt in them slammed into her like a fist to the gut.

"I wanted to stay," Mireille said.

A flare of green light pulsed out from Mireille's feet. For an instant, Rhia could see every minute crack and crevice carved into the firm dirt floor. A shiver of dust bucked up to knee height.

Rhia put a hand on the side of the well as the ground rocked beneath her.

"Mireille—" she said in warning, not sure what she was warning against.

"I did this." Mireille whispered. "This is what I wanted."

With a gasp of earth, one of the cell's dirt walls collapsed. Rhia's knees wobbled as a tremor shuddered through the earth around the wellhouse.

There was a horrible grinding crack, terribly loud and immediate, like being inside a bone as it fractured. Moonlight streamed into the wellhouse as a plank in the wall fell out.

The earth rattled again. There was a boom and a roof timber slammed into the ground two feet away from her. Rhia pitched hard to her left and fell over the guard wall and into the well.

Darkness swallowed her. Her hands flailed in front of her face in useless self-defense. The scent of mold and old stone was suffocating. In an instant, she was sure her neck would break on the dry well basin—

A gout of uprushing water smacked Rhia in the face. The texture of the darkness surrounding her changed substantially. Her descent slowed, stopped, reversed. Mineral-scented well water soaked her. She inhaled a lungful and was still coughing when it carried her over the edge of the well and deposited her on the wellhouse floor. When her eyes cleared, Tansin was sitting up next to her, swaying drunkenly back and forth, one hand outstretched toward the well. The puddle of muddy water they sat in glowed a vibrant tropical blue.

"A real soft one." Rhia remembered Creff describing Tansin's Talent. *"Probably only second or third degree."*

That was way more than a second or third degree trick. Rhia didn't have time to think about it. An ominous chatter of lumber and earth echoed through the room.

Another earthquake rocked the floor. She used it to roll up to her feet. Rhia seized Tansin around the waist and levered her upright.

"We have to get out of here!"

The woman was shaky as a new colt, but she knew where the door was and lurched toward it. Rhia grabbed a handful of Mireille's robes on the way and pulled her along behind. The air was full of dust, the earth jittering around her feet like it was alive with millions of bugs. Rhia threw them all at the wellhouse door, hoping the frame hadn't shifted and trapped them inside.

It hadn't. She flung herself out into the moonlight and stumbled across the sobbing earth. Behind them, the building screamed. When they were clear, Rhia fell to her knees, fists clenched in the dry grass, eyes screwed shut.

The shaking stopped.

She counted to five, tipped in a shuddering breath around the feeling that she might throw up, and opened her eyes.

Tansin was on one side of her, flat on her back, staring at the stars like she'd never seen them before. Her chest pulsed with fast, frightened breaths. On Rhia's other side, Mireille was climbing stiffly to her feet. When she was solidly upright, she walked back toward the wellhouse.

Rhia rose and followed.

The wellhouse was gone. The earth where it had stood was punctured by a sinkhole thirty feet across. As they watched, it filled with brackish water.

"I guess you unblocked the aquifer," Mireille said.

"I didn't do anything," Rhia said. Her voice was froggy from inhaled dust. "That was Tansin."

"Really?" The tension had drained out of Mireille's face, and she looked only vaguely interested.

Dust hung heavy in the air. The edge of the sinkhole was raw loam, a sharp contrast to the wellhouse's hard-packed earthen floor. Water licked thirstily at shattered wood beams. The hole was filling fast, as if the water had square footage it wanted to reclaim.

Rhia's mind jumped over to the dry spring back on the edge of town, its taproot so devoid of moisture it could have been ceramic. She had thought it at the time, thought it and not put it together: *Unnatural.*

She gestured at the growing pond. "Did you do this? Use your Talent, stop the water? Did you cause the drought, so the people here would need your help?"

"No!" Mireille shook her head hard. Her eyes were enormous. "I would never. Cerretour is dying because of this. I never wanted to hurt anyone."

Tansin emitted a dry, retching cough, drawing both their eyes. The woman was looking up at Rhia, but her gaze was loose and distended and Rhia couldn't tell if she could actually see her or not.

"She did it," Rhia said, realization dawning as she spoke. "It was Tansin. She stopped up the well hoping people would investigate. If they dug, maybe they would find her. She caused the drought."

"Her Talent isn't strong enough for that."

Rhia remembered the gout of water slapping her in the face, the torrential uprush of focused water carrying her out of the wellshaft. "Maybe it wasn't when you put her down there. But it sure is now."

"That's . . . that's miraculous." Mireille's face relaxed in a spasm of evaporating guilt. "Then it worked. The tempering worked. Praise the gods."

Later, the memory of Mireille's relief would be revolting. But right now, the adrenaline was wearing off and Rhia was shaky and tired. Her bones ached. When she spoke, her voice sounded like someone else was using it: "The wild world has room for all manner of things."

Rhia thought again that she should have been afraid, and couldn't manage it. Not of Mireille. Mireille, who had sat next to her on that barrel last night, laughing and swinging her feet like a child. Mireille, who had taken her to her home, made her dinner, prayed in front of her at her shabby altar. Mireille, who had emerged from behind the mantle of Priesthood and smiled at her beside the spring. Mireille, who had walked with her through the sunlight like they were sisters. Mireille, who had tried, in her own way, to be her friend.

The stars circled silver overhead. Standing out here on the edge of the world, they could have been the only people on the continent.

"Who are you, really?" Rhia asked.

"Me?" Mireille shook her head. "I'm no one. Just like you."

"Mireille . . ." Rhia didn't like the distance in the other woman's face. When she took Mireille's wrist, she had a flash of memory—the night she had arrived in Cerretour, again at the dry spring. Mireille had touched her the same way. "We should take Tansin back to town."

Mireille looked over the star-washed prairie. The few lights glowing in Cerretour made the town look like the last ship on a vast dark ocean. As Rhia watched, one of them broke loose from its anchor, bobbed down the road in their direction.

"They'll have heard the building come down," Mireille observed. "These poor people. I wanted to help them. I thought if Tansin's Talent developed enough, she would leave. Maybe they would need another Talent to replace her. If I could grow enough plants for them, even if we ended up having to abandon the town . . . maybe they'd want me. I wanted to *belong* with them. The way you belonged, when you were a child in the Temple. But I—I'm the thing they've been afraid of. I killed Rensoa—"

"It was an accident," Rhia said. She felt herself trying to steer the conversation down a narrow, precarious roadway. "Everyone will understand, Mireille. It was an accident."

"*You* don't understand." A tear dropped off the end of Mireille's nose—white in the moonlight—and spattered on her robe. "Rensoa was an accident. But this—" She gestured back at Tansin, still laying on the ground. "I could have told them weeks ago, but I didn't. I kept her here alone, in the dark, I hid her underground the entire time. I—I tortured her."

"I know."

"I lied. I lied about everything."

Something rustled in the grass, too near to be anyone coming out from town.

"Rhia." Mireille turned suddenly, took both Rhia's hands in hers. "Take a step back."

"What? Mireille—"

The woman squeezed Rhia's hands once and shoved her with tremendous strength, sending her onto her ass in the dirt. Rhia caught herself on her palms, wrists barking complaints. She peered up at Mireille, starting to ask what the hell—

Then the greyhowler came.

From her position on the ground, Rhia was at eye-level with it when it dug itself up. The dry grass around its body chattered as it shook free of the earth. The front half came up first, wide paws with long, bony toes and a backwards-pointing thumb. The shoulders were sharp and raw-boned, followed by a slatted ribcage, a heaving barrel. It came up with a rancid stench of blood and shit.

Two sulphur-colored eyes snapped onto Rhia's face, set forward in an unsettlingly flat skull. Its mouth was a long scythe curve that went back to the sharp leather curls of its ears, and when it hissed with the efforts of unburying itself, Rhia saw a row of knife-edged teeth. In the sound of its hiss, she heard the ghosts of the howls that had kept the town indoors all night. Its skin was a matte, hairless grey, the same unremarkable tone of the prairie at night. It had been right there—it had been there the *entire time*, it was *real*—and she hadn't known it.

It was less than six feet away from her. Rhia froze in place, wanting more than anything to scuttle backwards, but terrified of drawing its attention. She couldn't take her eyes off its hooked graphite-colored claws.

The earth shivered under Rhia's palms.

"Mireille!"

Boots pounded on the road. Will Cordance thundered into the clearing where the wellhouse had stood, a lantern bobbing on a ring in his hand, and for all Rhia had told him to stay away from her that afternoon, she was wildly grateful to see him now. She was facing a monster told of in Temple legend, and maybe a Temple Priest would know what to do about it.

He saw Rhia and the greyhowler at the same time and he went perfectly still.

"Mireille," he said to the woman in front of the slowly-filling pond. "This can stop."

"No it can't," Mireille said. The ground around her feet was glowing green for six feet in every direction. "I know the legend. The lusus mendace is the eater of lies."

The greyhowler turned its face to Mireille, which suggested an intelligence Rhia found freshly terrifying. Was it attracted to the sound of her voice, or had it recognized that she was talking about it?

"It's done its duty," Will said. "It brought me to you. We no longer need it."

Mireille shook her head.

Will said something in a dialect Rhia didn't know. It sounded like the ritual language used in the oldest Temple rites, but older, more primal—the rounded vowels replaced by harsher clipped ones.

The greyhowler's demeanor changed: the curve of its spine softened; its head tilted; it made a soft trilling complaint.

Will's voice took on a soothing tone.

The greyhowler put its chin on the ground between its paws.

"You can come back with us, Mireille," Will said. He used the same soothing tone, like he was still trying to comfort a wild animal. "I came from the Temple to find you. You don't have to keep running."

"No, I can't." Her voice was thick with tears. "I thought this was the place. I thought I could belong. But it's too late. I've done too much. It's too many lies."

"Mireille, don't," Rhia said. She felt the other woman stepping off the path she had tried to lay out for them, going in a terminal direction. She started to stand up.

The greyhowler's head whipped around. It was up on all fours in an eyeblink, its skin wrinkling into protective folds. Its lips peeled off jagged rows of teeth. Moving swift and low to the ground like a wildcat, it paced between the two women. A horrible chattering cry stuttered out of its mouth. Its eyes pinned Rhia in place.

Rhia's spine turned to ice. Every childhood story came thundering back and sat on her chest.

Don't look at me. Don't look at me. I'm not a liar, don't look at me—

The greyhowler's eyes were acid yellow, and they seemed to grow, engulfing her. She couldn't look away. The stench of old blood choked her.

"Hey," Mireille said. "Pay attention. I'm the one you came to eat."

The greyhowler's attention snapped onto the woman who wasn't an acolyte.

A slow rumble began to emanate out from under Mireille's feet. The water in the pond shivered, the reflected stars breaking into a jittering dance.

As Rhia watched, the earth around the Mireille softened and she began to sink.

"Mireille, *don't*—"

Will shouted something in that other language, but it was too late. A wet, rending growl boomed up from the greyhowler's throat.

All Rhia could see was starlight and gleaming teeth and Mireille's pale face, a heartbreaking reflection of the cold moon in the sky.

"I want to stay," she said clearly as she disappeared into the dark ground.

The monster plunged after her, its body arced in a deadly predatory curve.

Sunlight scraped a gold comb over the surface of the prairie. Rhia waited at the edge of the dry spring and watched the birds cut tight loops out of the grass. They swooped up and over, dramatic jags to the left or right, tethered to the ground by invisible strings. They snatched bugs out of the air above the prairie and shouted at each other about it. It was a riot of birdsong, and given the hour, she found it a little obnoxious.

Her pack sat beside her, fully loaded and ready to be borne away.

The grass on the other side of the spring shuddered. Rhia heard a splash. This was what she'd been waiting for. She sat up and watched.

They had unburied the length of pipe spanning between the wellhouse and the spring, carefully dug up and replaced sections that were crumbling or broken. This morning, Tansin had started working at the other end, where the new pond had formed at the site of the collapsed wellhouse.

A gout of clear water shot through the pipe and spattered into the dry spring. Sunlight crackled off the droplets.

Rhia bounced onto her feet and jumped down into the spring. She bent and pressed a palm to the wet earth, pulsed her Talent out. The taproot that had filled the spring basin from the aquifer was still there. Now that Tansin was back aboveground and the aquifer was unblocked, there was more water in the ground. It wouldn't happen overnight, but the spring should heal, begin to fill again. In the meantime, Tansin's Talent would pull a bit of water across the flat land, filling the spring from the wellhouse pond until it returned to normal levels.

The prairie sighed and Tansin slipped out of the grass beside the trough. She saw Rhia picking her wet boots out of the mud and smiled.

"Told you you could do it," Rhia said.

The other woman dashed sweat off her brow. "It was difficult. But you were right. I just thought about moving it an ounce at a time."

Tansin's blossoming Talent was a silent presence between them. They hadn't discussed the outcomes of Mireille's attempts to temper her, but after two weeks, the results seemed to be permanent.

In private, Will had told Rhia that the genuine fear of death sometimes provoked a person's Talent to stretch beyond its usual limits, but he'd also said a lot of stuff about the hands of the gods working constantly to make level the scales of the universe, and Rhia had kind of tuned him out.

"You're really coming along," she said to Tansin as she climbed out of the spring. "Will still trying to get you to go with him to Bywater?"

"Yeah." Dark hair bounced around her cheeks as Tansin shook her head. Despairing of getting all the mud out of it, she'd cropped it close to her chin. It curled out around her head in a thick corona. "I don't wanna, though. All those Priests. I'd rather . . . stay close to home for awhile."

"I get it."

"It's the least I can do," Tansin continued. "Given that I caused the spring to dry up to begin with . . . The town could use a water-finder, anyway. This won't be our last drought."

"Might be," Rhia said. She jerked her chin at the water filling the spring. "You keep pulling off tricks like that."

Tansin blushed and turned back into the grass, which folded as she tromped away, heading back to the pond.

She'd tended toward being taciturn already, Rhia gathered, and the time underground had only intensified it. Will said that almost every night, Tansin woke screaming from nightmares of darkness, stale air, the feeling of earth trickling down her throat. She didn't even like to be indoors more than necessary, preferring to spend most of her time outside by the spring. Rhia figured that was as good a farewell as any. She picked up her pack.

"Leaving already?"

Will stood at the end of the road, looking at her across the filling spring. He wore simple street clothes. She hadn't seen him in Priest robes since Rensoa's funeral.

Rhia shrugged. "Was gonna. Before it gets too hot."

He beckoned her over. "Stay a spell."

"A short spell," she cautioned as she maneuvered around the spring. "I have a long trip."

"I know. I'll be making my own way, soon enough. I figure I can stay a few more weeks, help Tansin get acquainted with her Talent. The Temple will support that."

Rhia came and stood beside him at the spring, close enough for conversation but too far away to touch. The last two weeks had seen an uneasy peace settle between them, but she was still wary. She hadn't forgiven him for lying, both about who he was and about his own belief in the greyhowler.

Rhia wondered if he'd seen Tansin depart. "She doesn't want to go back with you," she said. "She doesn't want to be a Priest anymore."

"I know." Will laced his fingers over his stomach and looked at the rivulet of water dripping into the spring. "It's a shame, but . . . I do understand. And if the Temple objects, well . . . I have enough sway that no one will come out and try to convince her."

"Who *are* you?" Rhia asked. "You travel incognito. You could speak to that monster . . . you're not just a Priest."

Will shrugged. "At my core, I am a Priest, but it is only one of the things I am. The Temple has a long tradition of people such as myself. There aren't many of us, however, and we don't tend to advertise."

"So you're what? You're a monster hunter?"

"What?" he chortled. "Gods, no. I'm a truth-seeker. The Temple uses me, and people like me, to search for . . . inconsistencies in the various manifestations of the faith."

"You hunt heretics."

"Sometimes." He smiled sadly. "Most recently, no. I hunted a woman who wanted to be a Priest.

"The Temple has known for some time that there was a woman out here in the wilds, an acolyte who had attempted her trials and failed them. She would never be a Priest, and she knew it. Usually the Temple finds other uses for such people, but before we could help her, she disappeared."

"Help her," Rhia snorted. "Why do I think you and I have really different definitions of that word."

"Believe what you like," Will said. "But my intentions were only ever to do good. Bring her home; keep her safe. She was out on the prairie by herself for months. She wasn't stable. She wasn't fit to be in the world without guidance. But she was still a powerful Earth Talent, and the Temple could have used her abilities.

"That's what was in the letter you carried to Micah, by the way. A warning to be watchful for an Earth Talent claiming to be on roving. We believe she applied at a number of local Temples and was always turned away. I assume that's why she disguised herself as an acolyte, rather than a full Priest. She knew she couldn't fake it convincingly."

Rhia shook her head. It was easy to look at behavior you didn't understand and call it madness, but it didn't sit right with her. "I still don't know what she was doing. Why she was here."

"Isn't it enough to say she wanted what we all want? To be seen, to be accepted, to be needed, to be loved? Mireille wanted to find her community. To make a family here. As far as we've been able to discover, she had none of her own."

The mention of the woman's name put a twist in Rhia's heart. In the halls of her memory, starlight picked out the curve of Mireille's cheek, turned her crown of braids into a silver wreath.

"I'm no one. Just like you."

She looked out into the tall grass, trying to distract herself. The tawny stalks swayed and she tracked the path of an animal through them. Probably a fox or a coyote. Maybe something else.

"Whatever was it, anyway?" she asked, trying to change the subject. "The monster. The greyhowler? The *lusus mendace*?"

"Different names for the same thing. One a Temple legend, one a folktale." Will didn't look at her. He was tracking the same jagged path through the grass. "When I said there aren't many Priests like me... the lusus mendace is a manifestation of my Talent. It happened when I assumed the Priesthood. It's my... gift. So to speak." He pulled down the loose collar of his shirt to display an asymmetrical white scar, bigger than Rhia's spread hand, roughly the shape of a star.

Horrified and fascinated, Rhia leaned closer. "It . . . was born from you?"

"More like erupted, but yes." He tugged his shirt back into position. "It was quite the experience."

Rhia couldn't stop staring at the spot on his chest where the monster had come from. It was right over his heart. "Gods have mercy."

Will chuckled ruefully. "It nearly killed me. Priesthood isn't for the weak-hearted. That's one of the reasons I think you'd make a great one."

"That night . . . you said it did its duty, bringing you to Mireille."

"You know the legends. The lusus mendace is a companion of truth-seekers, a guardian."

"So what, you were working with it? It brought you here?"

"Working with it? Not really. I can't command it, only observe. It goes, I follow. It's attracted to, among other things, heretics and grievous lies. When it lingers somewhere, I know it's found something, and I try to intervene, to make right before it strikes. I was already looking for an impersonator pretending to be an acolyte when the lusus mendace brought me here. I don't know if a lie like Mireille's assumed identity would have been enough to attract it, but imprisoning Tansin, tempering her, and pretending she was missing certainly was."

"Do you think it . . . found her?"

"Mireille?" Will sighed. "Impossible to say. Part of me thinks she must have died in the earth. Part of me thinks that with her Talent, she could have escaped it."

Rhia's bitter practicality argued against that idea. The greyhowler had moved with the speed and ease of a life-long hunter.

But she didn't want Mireille to be dead, didn't want to imagine her torn apart by a beast in the belly of the earth. She didn't want the other woman to have sacrificed herself, whether for Rhia or from the guilt of her own lies. "I don't even know what to hope for," Rhia confessed. "Even if she did escape somehow . . . it would go after her again. Wouldn't it?"

"I wouldn't be so quick to assume that," Will replied. "If the lusus mendace is the devourer of falsehood, Mireille would have to continue lying to draw its hunger. If she survived somehow, if she escaped . . . living an honest life would protect her from it. All she would have to do, when next given the opportunity, is remain her true self."

"Really?"

"Truly," he said. "I speak from experience. There are very few wrongs so terrible they can't be made right somehow."

"Wouldn't you rather it found her?" Rhia asked. "I'm sure you'd be happier to know there was one less heretic in the world."

"Courier, please. I have a heart." Will shook his head. "You know, most of my work is exposing con artists, fake messiahs, those who claim to be god-touched and use it to exploit true believers. Mireille . . . she wasn't that."

Rhia shook her head. She knew what it was like to be rejected, to lose your home. But where Rhia had repudi-ated the Temple, Mireille had built a lie that let her cling to it and buried Tansin in the foundation. "Good inten-tions don't excuse what she did."

"No, they don't. But if she were here to be held account-able by the people of Cerretour, perhaps her good inten-tions would save her." Will gave her an unsettlingly direct gaze. "Nothing's ever only one way, Rhia."

Don't talk to me like you know me, Priest. But she didn't say it, because he wasn't wrong.

"She's probably dead."

Will shrugged. "She may be. But as they say, hope is the only burden that lightens the heart."

He was right about that too.

The grass on the other side of the spring shuddered. A lanky, charcoal-colored animal shoved through it. Twin yellow eyes reflected in the rippling spring. All the birds fell silent. Rhia froze.

"It's no threat to us," Will said quietly. "We're not what it's hunting."

The greyhowler eased the rest of its long body out of the brush. It bent its flat face to the surface of the spring and lapped. Its tongue was surprisingly pink.

It drank intently for less than a minute, then vanished back into the grass.

The birds resumed their songs.

Rhia shook her head, still frightened, still amazed.

"The wild world has room for all manner of things."

"Exactly." Will touched her arm gently. "It's been an honor, Courier."

He lumbered down the road, heading for the shabby build-ings and knobby plants and slowly-growing lives in Cerretour.

Rhia turned away. For a long time, she stood looking at the opaque screen of prairie.

There was a potato bush growing on the side of the spring. It was blooming out of season. As Rhia bent to secure a bootlace that had come loose, the plant's star-shaped flowers brushed against her fingers. She imagined potatoes swelling in the earth.

She hoped Mireille was down there somehow, coaxing them to grow.

Her fingers lingered against the petals, then left them.

ACKNOWLEDGMENTS

The pressure to appreciate every person who's had any impact on my life as I publish my first book is immense. I won't be doing that; there are too many people to list and you don't want to read about them all. I'll just have to write more books and hope I get through all the important people before I die.

Here are some highlights:

The book you're reading would not have been possible without Mark Teppo's thoughtful, detailed feedback. Mark, thanks for taking a chance on my first book. I'm proud of it, and I hope you are too. Thanks for seeing Rhia so clearly and caring about her enough to coax more of her out onto the page. Thanks also for sending me a physical check for the advance, which gave me something nice to frame.

My parents, who have mastered the skill necessary to successful parenting: Inexhaustible enthusiasm for my pursuits, even when my personal brand of weirdness goes far beyond what either of them probably imagined for their child.

Monica, Rachel, and Chelsea: thank you for decades of much healthier friendship than the one that takes center stage in this book. (Monica, don't read it. It's too scary.)

Tim: Cheerleader, collaborator, co-conspirator, one of the great loves of my life. You believed in my writing before I did. I wouldn't be here, embarking on this big authorial adventure, without you. (Look, I did it!)

Brad: Some of me will always be on the dreamy green forest patio at that AirBnB in Guerneville, listening to Zorca's playlists and finishing the first draft of a story that became this novella, and some of you will always be there with me. I love you. I'd do it again in a heartbeat.

ABOUT THE AUTHOR

Sarah Day lives in the San Francisco Bay Area with her cat and entirely too many LED lights. She enjoys video games, lifting weights, and watching horror movies from behind the cracks between her fingers.

Her handle is @scribblingfox pretty much everywhere online (except Instagram, where it's @scribbling.fox).

Keep up with her work at sarahday.org.